CAT
ON A
COLD TIN
ROOF

AN ELI PAXTON MYSTERY

CAT ON A COLD TIN ROOF

MIKE RESNICK

SEVENTH STREET BOOKS®
AN IMPRINT OF PROMETHEUS BOOKS
59 JOHN GLENN DRIVE • AMHERST, NY 14228
www.seventhstreetbooks.com

Published 2014 by Seventh Street Books®, an imprint of Prometheus Books

Cover image © Media Bakery
Cover design by Nicole Sommer-Lecht

Inquiries should be addressed to
Seventh Street Books
59 John Glenn Drive
Amherst, New York 14228
VOICE: 716–691–0133
FAX: 716–691–0137
WWW.SEVENTHSTREETBOOKS.COM

18 17 16 15 14   5 4 3 2 1

Library of Congress Cataloging-in-Publication Data

Resnick, Michael D.
    Cat on a cold tin roof : an Eli Paxton mystery / by Mike Resnick.
        pages cm
    ISBN 978-1-61614-889-8 (pbk.)
    ISBN 978-1-61614-890-4 (ebook)
    1. Private investigators—Ohio—Cincinnati—Fiction. 2. Murder—Investigation—Fiction. 3. Drug traffic—Fiction. I. Title.

PS3568.E698C38 2014
813'.54—dc23

2014006856

Printed in the United States of America

To Carol, as always,
and to Chip Hossler, Crown Prince of the Geek Squad

1.

They say Cincinnati is in the Upper South. They say the winters are mild. They say it hardly ever snows.

Clearly they don't remember the Ice Bowl in 1982, when the Bengals won the AFC Championship in a minus-59 wind chill. Or if they were too young for that, all they had to do was look out my apartment window, always assuming that white was their favorite color. We'd had six inches during the day, with more coming.

I had other problems than the weather. No clients for more than a week was first and foremost among them. Either no one needed a detective, or, more likely, they didn't need one urgently enough to brave the weather and come to my office. And the beat-up Ford needed a new transmission, which was going to set me back a couple of thousand, once I got my hands on a couple of thousand to be set back.

I was sitting on my well-used couch in front of the television, watching—or mostly dozing through—an endless series of Falcon movies on Turner Classic Movies, with George Sanders turning into Tom Conway somewhere along the way, and wondering why the Falcon never lacked for clients *or* money. After a while I stopped dozing and began sleeping in earnest.

I dreamed that I was on a beach with Sophia Loren, who had magically lost about fifty years, and was kissing my ear. "Ah, Sophia, my sweet!" I whispered. It encouraged her, and she began kissing my ear more vigorously.

After another few seconds she began drooling in my ear and then growling in it, and I woke up and realized that she had morphed into Marlowe, my dog. They say he's a West Highland White Terrier, but he hasn't been white since the day I got him. I don't like him much, and he likes me even less. But he has no more luck with lady dogs than I have with lady people, so we stay together.

It was only when he began barking, maybe an inch from my ear, maybe a little less, that I realized the phone was ringing. I looked at my watch: three in the morning.

Nobody calls me at three in the morning, especially during a blizzard, so I let it ring seven or eight times until it finally stopped, found that the Falcon had gone the way of all flesh, and I was now watching Chester Morris as Boston Blackie and had just about gone back to sleep when the phone began ringing again, and Marlowe barked in my ear about a tenth of a second later.

I brushed Marlowe off my shoulder, where he'd been sleeping before he began barking, got up, and trudged to the phone.

"Yeah?" I said, picking it up.

"Hi, Eli. It's Jim Simmons. I tried to call a minute ago, but I must have dialed a wrong number. Nobody goes out on a night like this."

"Nobody except cops," I answered. Jim was my closest friend on the Cincinnati police.

"True, true," he said.

"Okay," I said. "You didn't call me at three in the morning to talk about the Bengals."

"They looked really good last Sunday, didn't they?" he said. "Or at least not as bad as usual. But no, that's not it. I'm calling from the Grandin Road area." That's Cincinnati's answer to LA's Malibu or Chicago's Lake Shore Drive. "There's been a murder."

I frowned. "I'm sorry to hear it, but why the hell are you calling *me*? You've got a billion dollars' worth of stuff in your forensics lab, and God knows how many men on the force. Private detectives haven't been hired to solve murders since Sam Spade retired."

"I know."

"Well, then?"

"Shut up and listen," he said. "We'll take care of the murder. But something's missing, something that probably has nothing to do with the murder. The lady of the house—I guess I should call her the widow, since that's what she's been for an hour or two—wants to hire a detective to get it back, and it's a field in which you seem to have specialized."

A field in which I've specialized? What the hell was that?

"If I give you the address, can you get here in twenty minutes?" continued Simmons.

"Jim, I don't even know if I can get to my car in twenty minutes," I answered. "Have you stuck your head out a window?"

"Damn it, Eli! I drove here myself! The plows are keeping up with it."

My first inclination was to say no. Then I figured he'd press me, and I'd tell him my transmission was on borrowed time. Then I figured, well, Grandin Road, what the hell, maybe this'll pay for it.

"All right," I said. "Give me the address, and I'll be there as soon as I can . . . but I guarantee it's going to take more than twenty minutes."

"That's okay," said Simmons. "Just so's you get here. The rest of us aren't going anywhere."

I wrote down the address. "I never heard of the street. How the hell do I get there?"

"Just tell your GPS where you're going."

"What's a GPS?"

"I forgot which century you're living in," said Simmons. "It figures that anyone who doesn't have a cell phone doesn't have a GPS. OK, go east on . . ."

He rattled off the directions, I scribbled them down, and then I hung up. I never wear a gun, but I pulled it out of the drawer and strapped on the shoulder holster, just in case my client watched all the same movies I watch. I was going to explain to Marlowe that I had to go out, and that his food was in his bowl in the kitchen, but he'd figured it out already and was snoring peacefully on my couch.

I got into my coat and galoshes—I suppose they're boots these days, but they *feel* like galoshes—and made my way to the car. No one had bothered shoveling the sidewalk, but the plows were out in force on the streets. So was the snow, and it was going to be a near thing to see which emerged victorious. Personally, my money was on the snow, but

I hadn't had a client in a week, so I got into the car, was mildly surprised when it started right off the bat, waited a minute while it warmed up, and I stopped shivering and finally edged out into the street.

Ordinarily there were at least a few cars out, even at three in the morning, but except for the plows I seemed to be the only person crazy enough to be on the street. I set off at maybe twenty miles an hour, skidded a couple of times, and slowed down to twelve miles an hour.

I hoped Jim's instructions were accurate, because every street sign was covered with snow, except for the few that were covered by ice. I crossed over Interstate 71, saw a bunch of flashing lights and what seemed to be a four-car pile-up, tried not to think about it, and kept heading east.

The Grandin Road area—I'm sure it has a classier name, but I've never spent enough time over there to learn it—is a couple of square miles filled to the brim with huge, elegant Tudor and Georgian mansions, each more impressive than the last, each expensively landscaped, just a few miles from downtown Cincinnati. You get the feeling that entire mahogany forests were decimated just to supply the wainscoting and window frames for the few hundred houses that lined the twisting streets.

Nobody parks on the street around there, not with every house sporting a three- or four-car garage—but if they did, there'd be an endless row of luxury sedans of which the Lincoln Town Cars and Cadillac Escalades were the poor cousins. I had a feeling that I was getting close to my destination, but all the mailboxes, which were up at the head of the driveways, were so covered with snow that I couldn't read the addresses—and if any of the houses had addresses on or above the front doors I couldn't see them from the street.

Then I saw a drive with five cop cars parked in it, a couple of them with their lights still flashing, and I figured to hell with the address, how many houses have got five cop cars in their driveways at three in the morning with a blizzard raging? So I pulled up—they'd left me just enough room to get my car off the street and out of the way of the plows—parked, got out of the car, and tried not to slip on the ice while walking to the front door. The drive was lined with snow-covered shrubbery and towering oaks and maples, all of them glistening white in the moonlight.

I pressed the button, heard a musical chime, and a few seconds later a uniformed cop opened the door.

"Yes?" he said, eyeing me suspiciously.

"Eli Paxton," I said, waiting for him to step aside so I could get in out of the cold.

He stared at me without moving.

"Jim Simmons sent for me," I explained.

He looked suspicious. "Wait here," he said. "I'll check with Officer Simmons."

He began closing the door, but I stuck my foot in before he could shut it.

"It's freezing out here," I said. "Why don't you just pull your gun on me and march me to wherever the hell Simmons is?"

He stared at me again, then shrugged, stepped aside, and gestured for me to enter.

"Take off your boots," he said.

The tile on the foyer practically glowed and looked like it cost more than the average house—and hanging down from the ceiling about forty feet above me was a crystal chandelier that I imagined wouldn't have looked out of place in Buckingham Palace. I took my boots off.

"May I ask what your business is, sir?"

I shrugged. "Beats the hell out of me. Jim Simmons phoned an hour ago and told me to get the hell over here."

He arched an eyebrow. "An hour?"

"You try driving through that shit," I said.

He grunted, muttered, "Follow me," and headed to the broad, winding staircase, the kind that Fred Astaire and Ginger Rogers would dance down with a couple of chorus girls on each side of them.

"Uh . . . is there someplace I can leave my coat?" I said, as the house was quite warm and comfortable, which meant that I was feeling warmer and more uncomfortable by the second.

He shook his head. "You'll need it."

I frowned. What the hell was I going to need my coat for?

"Come on," he continued, starting to climb the stairs again. We passed four beautifully framed oil paintings that were hanging on the walls as we ascended. I didn't know who'd done them, but I'd have bet my bottom dollar he or she was pretty damned famous if you knew expensive art. That left me out, as my own taste in art was pretty much limited to Playmates and old pulp magazine covers.

As we reached the top of the stairs the cop turned left, and I saw half a dozen more uniformed cops lining the forty-foot corridor. The double door at the end of it was open, leading to a huge master suite, and my guide headed off toward it.

He stopped at the doorway, held up a hand to indicate I was to stop too, and he called out, "Officer Simmons?"

A moment later Jim Simmons, looking elegant compared to me but a little rumpled compared to the other plainclothesmen, walked over to me.

"Hi, Eli. I'd ask what kept you, but I was just standing outside a minute ago."

"Must be another staircase," I said. "I know this one's big, but I never saw you come up."

He smiled grimly. "Come on in," he said, turning and walking into the suite, which was about twice the size of my entire apartment, with a four-poster bed that could have accommodated a small army.

"It's cold in here," I noted.

"Door's open," replied Simmons.

"Door?"

He nodded and pointed to a sliding door that led out to what looked like a deck.

"What's all this about, Jim?" I asked.

"Like I said on the phone," he replied, "there's been a murder. Ever hear of Malcolm Pepperidge?"

I shook my head. "If this is his house, I suspect we traveled in different social circles."

"Not quite as different as this place makes it seem," said Simmons.

"I had a feeling you never heard of Pepperidge. How about Big Jim Palanto?"

"Sounds like a wrestler or a mobster," I replied.

Simmons nodded. "Close. He was the financial advisor to Chicago's biggest Mafia family, the man who invested their money for them." He paused, pulled out a thin, Clint Eastwood spaghetti Western cigar, considered it for a few seconds, then frowned and put it back in his pocket. "Trying to quit," he explained. "Anyway, Palanto never broke the law himself, but he knew most of the mob's secrets, and he decided to walk away from the business while he was still alive. That was about fifteen years ago. He came away with an estimated ten million, and since he knew how to invest it, he's probably worth two or three times that today."

"Okay," I said. "Pepperidge is dead and Palanto is rich. What's the connection?"

"Palanto *became* Pepperidge when he left the mob and moved here. He's been a model citizen ever since."

"Then it wasn't the mob that hit him?"

"Of course it was," said Simmons.

I frowned. "I'm missing something here. I thought you said he came away clean and stayed clean."

"He did," replied Simmons. "But some of his old buddies have a trial coming up, and he was subpoenaed to testify against them. It figures they were just making sure he couldn't show up. After all, how loyal could he be after fifteen years?"

"If he's worth ten million or more, all thanks to them, and no one can prove the money's dirty after all this time, what could he gain by siding with the prosecution?" I asked.

"Probably nothing," said Simmons. "But if you were up for seven murders and half a hundred other felonies, would you take the chance on someone who cut out fifteen years ago?"

I exhaled deeply. "No, I suppose it makes sense."

"We haven't got much time to catch the guy," added Simmons. "They'd never use a local shooter. He'll be out of town the second the roads are clear or the airport re-opens."

"They probably wouldn't send one of their own from Chicago, either," I agreed. "If you're right about who's behind it, they probably imported one from either coast."

Simmons nodded. "Yeah, I know."

"Okay," I said. "I know who got killed, I know who he really was, and I probably know why he was killed. What I don't know is what *I'm* doing here at four in the morning in the middle of the worst blizzard of the year."

"The grieving widow's got a job for you."

"What kind of a job?"

"Follow me for a minute," he said, heading off toward the sliding doors. He pulled one aside and stepped out onto the balcony, where two uniformed cops and two homicide detectives were already gathered.

"The balcony wasn't originally part of the house," continued Simmons. "It's just a tin roof over the garage. But about four years ago he became interested in astronomy, so he had the sliding doors put in, and covered the tin with some kind of decking. We won't know exactly what kind until the damned snow melts—not that it matters anyway."

The cops had roped it off, which didn't make much sense, since it was fifteen or twenty feet above the ground. But they'd also put a tarp over the top of it at a height of maybe eight feet, as if to stop the snow from covering up any evidence. It was already starting to sag from the weight.

Stretched out face-down on the balcony, right next to a telescope that had been attached to the railing, was the dead man.

"We hate to leave him like this," said one of the detectives, "but the forensics guys asked us to keep the scene pristine until they got here." He chuckled sardonically. "Pristine!" he repeated, shaking his head. "That tarp's gonna collapse under the weight of the snow in another twenty minutes or so."

"So where are they?" I asked.

"Sleeping, at least 'til we called them," was the reply. "This isn't Chicago, with three or four murders a day. I doubt we average as many as one a week."

"As you can see," Simmons said, pointing to the corpse, "all he's got on is his robe, his pajamas, a pair of unbuckled boots, and an overcoat that he threw on to protect himself from the cold. According to his wife and his staff, he was an avid stargazer. There are two bullets in his back. Clearly the killer nailed him while he was looking at something, though what the hell he could see in this snowstorm is beyond me."

"According to the weather reports, it let up from one-thirty to almost two o'clock, sir," said one of the uniformed men. "It's up to the coroner to fix the time of death if he can, but it's a fair guess that he came out during the pause in the storm to see if it was done or if there was more coming."

"Makes sense," agreed Simmons. "I don't know if it's right, but it makes sense."

I looked for a long moment as the wind whipped across the balcony, then started getting very cold. "Okay," I said, "I've seen him. I've seen the balcony. I've seen the bedroom. And I still don't know what this has to do with me."

"Take a closer look," said Simmons.

"At what?"

He pointed to some small tracks around the corpse's head, leading to the edge of the balcony.

I looked and I shrugged. "Squirrel?" I suggested, but I knew that made no sense. Why would a squirrel leave the safety of a tree to leap onto an open balcony in a snowstorm?

"Cat," said Simmons.

"So where is it?" I asked, looking around.

"Beats the hell out of me."

I took another look at Pepperidge. There wasn't much blood, but if the bullets had gone through him, gravity was probably pulling it out of the exit wounds. And if not, well, maybe he died instantly, the heart wasn't pumping any blood after a few seconds, and it was pooled somewhere inside his body. I shrugged; it wasn't my business anyway.

Which reminded me that I *did* have some business to transact, no one had told me what it was yet, and I was freezing my ass off.

I turned to Simmons. "Okay, you got a dead man. But you also got a bunch of cops and detectives, and probably more on the way, plus a top-notch forensics crew—so what am I here for?"

"It's Mrs. Pepperidge," replied Simmons.

"Oh?"

He nodded. "She was playing in a bridge tournament all evening, and is the one who found the body."

"So?"

He smiled. "I think I'll let her tell you."

"Is she in any condition to talk?" I asked. "I mean, she just lost her husband."

"Tough broad," said Simmons. "If I was a betting man . . ."

"You are," I interrupted.

"Only on horses and football," he answered. "Anyway, if I was inclined to bet on people, I'd say that she has a lot more in common with the Chicago Palantos than the Cincinnati Pepperidges."

"Somehow I don't picture mob girls playing in bridge tournaments," I said.

"She hasn't been a girl in thirty years, and the tournament just shows that she's good at adapting to her surroundings."

"Okay, she's not a teenager, if she was ever a floozy she outgrew it, and she likes to play bridge."

"She likes cats, too," added Simmons.

"Fine," I said. "She likes cats too."

"Come on," he said, walking through the massive room and heading to the hallway.

I followed him, we walked past three empty rooms and still more paintings by artists who were probably known to everyone who could afford a house like this, and came to a closed door with a uniformed cop standing guard. Simmons knocked on it.

"Mrs. Pepperidge?" he said.

"Come in," said a strong female voice, stronger that I'd have expected from a newly widowed woman.

He opened the door, and I followed him into a paneled study with a carpet so thick you got the feeling they had to mow it every few days. She was sitting at an antique wooden desk, drinking from an expensive-looking glass while an even more expensive-looking bottle sat on the desk next to her.

She was maybe five-foot-five or six, and she may have been slim and sexy once, but these days she looked more like a linebacker. She wore a tailored pantsuit, her face had been lifted at least once and probably a couple of times, and her auburn hair had some beautiful white streaks through it. I don't know from hair, but I'd have bet whatever my fee for this gig was that those weren't its real colors. The most lasting impression was that she wore enough gold and diamond jewelry to make your pupils contract once the light hit them.

She looked me up and down, and finally got to her feet.

"I am Evangeline Pepperidge," she said, almost hiding the Chicago twang from her voice. "And you are . . . ?"

"Paxton, ma'am," I said, extending my hand. "Eli Paxton. I want to offer my condolences for your loss."

She looked at my hand as if it was diseased, and finally I let it drop to my side.

"Mr. Simmons has recommended you," she said.

"Lieutenant Simmons," Jim corrected her.

She glared at him for a moment, then turned back to me.

"Are you available to begin work immediately, Mr. Paxton?"

"First thing in the morning," I assured her.

"I said *immediately*," she repeated harshly.

"Yes, ma'am," I replied. "Immediately."

"Good. I'm not going to quibble about your fee. This is much too important." She reached down behind the desk, opened a drawer, pulled out a wad of bills, and handed it to me.

"That's fifteen hundred dollars, Mr. Paxton," she said. "It will serve as your retainer. I will pay you two hundred dollars a day plus all expenses while you are working for me, and a thousand-dollar bonus when you successfully complete your assignment."

Yeah, I decided, *it was worth coming out in the snow.* My usual fee was a hundred and a half a day, and as often as not I let it be negotiated downward when I was hard up for clients, which was usually the case. As for the retainer, it was the biggest I'd seen in three years.

"I assume these terms are acceptable?" she said when I was still doing the math and seeing how soon I could get the Ford its transmission.

"Perfectly, Mrs. Pepperidge, ma'am," I said.

"Good," she said, opening another desk drawer, pulling out a bunch of four-by-six photos, and handing them to me.

I thumbed through them. It was a normal, unexceptional-looking cat. A mackerel tabby, I think they call it, with a distinctive white spot over its left eye. It was lying on the dead man's lap in a couple of them.

"Looks like a cat," I said.

"Of course she's a cat!" she snapped. "*My* cat."

"Okay," I said. "It's your cat. What's its name?"

"*Her* name is Fluffy," she said somewhat distastefully. "My husband named her." She paused. "She's gone missing, and I want her back."

I had an almost irresistible urge to tell her that what she wanted was an animal warden, not a detective. Then I thought about the transmission and the overdue rent, and managed to resist the urge after all.

"We know from the prints that she was on the roof when her husband . . . when . . . ah . . ." said Simmons uncomfortably.

"I want that cat back, Mr. Paxton," she said, ignoring Simmons. She handed me a card. "The top number is my cell phone, the bottom is my landline. I'll expect a daily progress report. Mr. Simmons tells me that you once found a missing show dog."

"True," I replied. I decided not to tell her that the dog was dead when I found it a couple of thousand miles from home.

"Good. I assume that this is your *métier*." She pulled one more sheet of paper out of the desk while I was trying to figure out what a *métier* was. "This is the phone number and address of her vet, and below it is the kennel we board her at when we're abroad."

"Thank you," I said. I wondered what the odds were of finding a very small, nondescript cat in very deep snow, especially in the dark. A

thousand-to-one against sounded about right. "That spot above its—
her—eye should make her easy enough to identify."

"Well?" she demanded. "You're on my payroll now. Get to work."

I nodded and began backing out of the room. "Yes, ma'am. And let
me say once more how sorry I am about your husband."

"Forget him!" she yelled, all trace of wealthy Cincinnati sophistica-
tion departed. "Just find the fucking cat!"

2.

I figured I'd better look busy while I was still within sight of the upstairs window, so I pulled a flashlight out of my car, went back below the balcony, and started looking for the cat, or at least some cat tracks.

Dumb idea. You know how long an eight- or ten-pound cat's footprints last in a blizzard that's dumping an inch an hour on the ground? Neither do I, but it sure as hell isn't long.

I hung around, shining my light under every bush and in every possible hiding place, and after about twenty minutes in that weather I figured if I saw the cat camped out in some place that was warm and dry I'd join her, but of course only idiot detectives were out looking for cats they'd never seen before in the middle of a blizzard. Wherever the hell the cat was, I'd bet my bottom dollar that she was warm, dry, and someplace that surely qualified as "inside."

When I couldn't stand it any longer I went to my car, started the motor, waited until it heated up a bit, then turned the lights on, carefully backed out of the driveway—or where I thought the driveway *was*—and headed home. The plows were still working overtime, and the streets were actually a bit better than they'd been on the way over. I assumed that meant the snow was letting up, but you couldn't prove it by looking through the windshield.

I crossed over Interstate 71, kept heading west, finally came to my street, wished as I did every time it rained or snowed that I had a garage (or maybe a limo and a chauffeur), and pulled into the parking space I'd vacated a few hours earlier, reasonably grateful that nobody'd been suicidal enough to try driving down the street and parking since I'd left.

I locked the car, not that there was anything in it worth stealing, and climbed up the stairs to my apartment. I figured the least Marlowe could do was give a warning growl when he heard footsteps in the hallway, but instead all I could hear was contented snoring.

I unlocked the door, walked inside, realized I'd left the television on, and saw Marlowe snoring to Lloyd Nolan shooting off wisecracks and bullets as Michael Shayne.

"I'm home," I muttered.

Marlowe opened one eye, stared at me disapprovingly for a few seconds, and went back to sleep.

"I'm thrilled to see you too," I said, and went off to the kitchen for a beer, but when I opened the fridge and laid my hand on the can of Bud I realized that both of us—me and the can—were damned cold, which was fine if you were a beer but less so if you were me, so I put the beer back and started making a cup of coffee. Of course, by the time it was ready I'd warmed up and wanted a beer again, but since I'd just poured the coffee I sighed and began drinking it.

I knew if I flopped down on the bed I'd fall asleep, and if I got seven or eight hours I'd probably get fired for showing up at noon or one o'clock to continue the search, so I sat down on the couch instead.

"Shove over," I muttered. (Marlowe and I had been having a two-year battle about which of us had squatter's rights to the beat-up leather couch, which was the only comfortable piece of furniture in the place). Finally he grudgingly moved over a (very) few inches, decided to pretend I didn't exist, and went back to watching Michael Shayne out-smart the bad guys.

I envied him—Shayne, not Marlowe. Nobody dragged *him* out of bed at three in the morning. No one showed *him* a freshly killed mafioso and then told him to go find a cat in a snowstorm. No one expected him to look for a small, dark animal he'd never seen before on a large dark piece of property, armed only with a gun that he couldn't use on the cat and a flashlight that had seen better days and certainly brighter ones. And the worst part of the comparison was that Michael Shayne *always* got the girl. Of course, so did the Saint and the Falcon and Boston Blackie. And Nick Charles started out with the girl, which was possibly less romantic but also a hell of a lot less time-consuming. Me, I had an ex-wife I hadn't seen in years, a lady dog show judge who liked Marlowe better than me, and a lady cop from Kentucky who decided that shooting bad guys was more satisfying than smooching with a Cincinnati detective.

I was still feeling sorry for myself, or perhaps outraged at everything except myself, when I finally dozed off. I don't know how long I slept, three or four hours maybe, when suddenly I opened my eyes. I didn't know why for a moment, but I felt something was—I hate to say "amiss"—but at least not quite right.

And I realized that Marlowe was standing on the couch, his nose about four inches from mine, staring intently at me with an expression that said, "We have to go outside—*now!*"

I checked my watch. It was nine in the morning. "All right, all right, keep your shirt on," I growled as Marlowe continued to stare at me and thoughtfully made no reference to the fact that he wasn't wearing a shirt. I was still in my clothes, so I got into my shoes, galoshes and coat, attached a leash to his collar, and took him outside. Made it with about eight seconds to spare.

"You know," I mused as we began walking along in the morning sun, with him sticking his nose in the snow every couple of steps even though it damned near came up to his chest, "I'll bet you'd be better at spotting a cat than I would. At least you could bring one more sense to bear."

His entire attitude seemed to say: *Don't bother me when I'm doing whatever it is I'm doing when I keep burying my nose in the snow*, so I just kept walking along with him wherever he was going and trying to wake up and ignore the cold. And of course where he was going was Mrs. Garabaldi's petunias, which hadn't bloomed in months and were totally covered by snow anyway, and he lifted his leg where he thought they were, like he'd done every day since I'd got him, and even though it'd be another few months before the petunias began growing again, Mrs. Garabaldi stuck her head out of her window and began cursing at both of us in Italian, just like she always did. I resisted the urge to yell, "Marlowe says hello!" and kept walking.

Marlowe finally got chilly and began pulling me back to the apartment while I uttered a silent prayer of gratitude that he wasn't a collie or a Saint Bernard or something that *liked* the cold. As we neared the place he tugged me toward the door, but I figured I'd better get to work—or, more important, *be seen* getting to work—so I tugged him toward the car, and since I outweigh the little bastard by maybe a hundred and seventy pounds or so, I won (though not without a struggle).

I put the key in the ignition, turned it, and it took four tries for the damned thing to start. Then I realized that I hadn't scraped the snow off the windshield or any of the windows, so I waited for the car to warm up, turned the heat on high and the defroster on full blast, waited a couple of more minutes, and then got the scraper and brush and had the windows cleaned off in under a minute.

The snow had stopped while Michael Shayne was molesting the bad guys and grabbing the heroine, or maybe it was the other way around, and the plows had finished their work, at least temporarily. It took me about twenty minutes to get to the Pepperidge house. A trio of cop cars were still there, I checked to see if the cat had shown up, nobody seemed to know one was even missing, so I left Marlowe in the car, walked inside, started climbing the stairs, was told that this was a police inquiry and private eyes weren't welcome, determined that Jim Simmons had gone home to bed, explained what I was doing there, and asked them to send someone upstairs and make sure the cat was still missing.

I could hear Evangeline Pepperidge bellow through two or three closed doors that yes the goddamned cat was still missing, and an officer, looking like a young priest who had just mortally offended the pope, came to the head of the stairs and explained to me that I was still on salary.

I thanked him, went back outside, opened the back door so Marlowe could hop out, and walked him over to the area just beneath the balcony.

"Okay," I said. "Do your thing."

Maybe I should have worded it differently, because he proceeded to do his thing, then began pulling me back to the car.

I pulled back and began walking him around the area where the cat had to have landed. It was new territory to him, so he stuck his nose to the ground—or at least as close to the ground as the snow allowed—and began sniffing like there was no tomorrow.

I looked up and saw a cop looking down at me through the sliding glass door. There was no sign of my employer, but at least she knew I was on the job, and I figured I was as close to her right here as I cared to be.

Suddenly Marlowe began growling deep in his throat and began pulling me toward the back of the property. The going there was slower, since no one had plowed, shoveled, or even walked through the snow, but we made some progress. Then he froze, and just as I was wondering what the hell he had seen he began barking, and a dark cat shot out of *some*where and raced up a barren tree, reaching an icy branch and staring down at us.

"Damn!" I muttered, because now that I could see it clearly it was a plain brown, not a tabby of any kind, and more to the point, it didn't have that distinctive white spot over its left eye.

Still, Marlowe had either figured out what we were here for, or else he just liked terrifying anything smaller than himself, so I decided we'd scout around a little longer . . . but two hours later we hadn't run into anything except an occasional squirrel that was crazy enough to be out in the snow.

I decided to look a little farther afield, but after four servants—the owners were too busy to be bothered with such trivialities—told me to get the hell off their property, I figured I needed a different strategy before Simmons had to bail me out of Trespassers' Prison.

I led Marlowe back to the car, started the engine, and began driving slowly around the area, looking for the occasional stray cat, but it was a futile undertaking. Maybe it would have worked in the summer, but not with a foot of snow on the ground. Besides, even if I'd spotted one, even if it was a mackerel tabby, there was no way I could tell from a moving car if it had a white spot over an eye.

"Marlowe," I said, "I think your minutes as a full partner are limited. We're going home."

He showed his appreciation by growling and trying to dig a hole in the middle of the backseat.

I got home, put him back in the apartment, and looked up the SPCA headquarters in the phone book. Then I realized I hadn't eaten, so I slapped a little peanut butter on a piece of bread, decided it didn't look filling enough to substitute for breakfast *and* lunch, so I slapped some salami on it, and then some cream cheese, and then some grape jelly and a couple of apple slices, stuck another piece of bread on top of it, and carried it with me to the car, munching away and wondering why I hadn't just gone to a Skyline Chili joint instead.

I drove over to the SPCA and was greeted by a middle-aged lady who took a quick peek over my shoulder to see if I had a stray animal in the car that I was going to foist off on her.

"May I help you?" she asked.

I flashed my detective's license. Most people just take one look and assume I'm a cop and tell or give me whatever I want. Not this lady. She grabbed my hand as I was pulling it back and held it steady while she read every word of the tiny print.

"It expires in five weeks," she noted.

"Yeah, I know," I said, though of course I'd had no idea until she said so.

"So how may I help you, Detective Paxton, or is it just Mr. Paxton?"

"It's just plain Eli," I told her. "I've been retained to find a missing pet."

"It must be worth quite a lot, for them to hire a detective," she said.

"I have no idea about the pet," I replied. "But the *owner* is worth quite a lot."

She smiled. "And you are hoping that someone found it and turned it in?"

"If it didn't freeze to death," I said. "It's a very small cat."

"And it got out during last night's storm?"

I nodded.

"Poor thing!" she said.

"I have some photos of it," I said, pulling them out of a pocket. "As you can see, she's got a pretty distinctive mark over her left eye. Has anyone brought her in?"

She shook her head. "Nobody's turned in any cat at all during the past day."

"Damn!" I muttered. "Pardon my language, ma'am."

"I've heard worse," she assured me.

"Anyway, I guess I go back to looking behind bushes and under porches in her neighborhood."

"Not necessarily," she said.

"Oh?" I said. It wasn't much of a straw to grab at, but I wasn't in much of a position to be choosy.

"There are half a dozen animal shelters in the area," she replied. She reached behind a counter and pulled out a printed sheet of paper. "This is a list of them."

"Thanks," I said, studying the list. "One of them's only a mile from where the cat lived. I'll try that first."

"Just a moment, Mr. . . . Eli," she said.

"Ma'am?"

"Give me those photos for a moment. We have a color copier here. I'll run them off and leave a note that if she should turn up here, we're to call you."

"That's very thoughtful of you, ma'am," I said, handing her the pictures.

She took them, went into the next room, I could hear the copy machine going to work, and maybe two minutes later she emerged and handed them back to me.

"Thank you," I said.

"I need your cell phone number," she said, pen at the ready.

"My cell phone's on the blink," I lied. "I'll have to give you my home number."

"How about your office number, as long as you're on a case?"

"I work alone, I'm on a job, and it could be two or three days before I fight my way through this snow to get to my office." *Or two or three weeks before I catch up with the rent and the phone bill.*

"All right," she said, scribbling down the number as I gave it to her. "Good luck."

"Thanks for your help, ma'am," I said, walking out of the building.

I went to the car, considered stopping for a couple of cheese coneys or a four-way, decided that "breakfast" was filling enough and that the last thing I wanted to look at was food, and drove back to the east side of town, to the likeliest of the animal shelters.

I walked in, prepared to show the photos, and found that I didn't have to, that no cat had been brought in for the past three days.

Okay, so it wasn't in the house, it wasn't in the yard, it wasn't at the SPCA headquarters, and it wasn't in the closest, likeliest shelter. So what the hell was my next move? Cincinnati's not the biggest town in the world, Chicago's probably twice its size, even Cleveland's bigger, but I remembered reading that one deer could hide from a pair of hunters on one wooded acre, so how the hell was I going to find a small cat in a modern city, especially one where 90 percent of the surface was covered by maybe a foot of snow?

And how many more days, or even hours, could I spend looking for it before the bombastic Mrs. Pepperidge fired me and maybe decided I hadn't earned my money and refused to pay me?

I looked at the list. Five more shelters to go.

And when they all turned up negative, what then? I couldn't even blame the weather. What if the snow all vanished? Hell, there were probably thousands of stray cats roaming the streets and alleys and yards.

For a moment I wondered if Mrs. Pepperidge would take Marlowe as a replacement. Then I sighed, started the car again, and headed off to the next shelter.

3.

I got to see a lot of Cincinnati in the next day and a half, most of it covered with snow and ice. Every shelter assured me that they hadn't taken in any cats in the past two days, or at least not one with a white spot over its eye, and every shelter did its damnedest to convince me I'd be just as happy with one of the cats currently in residence. Even after I explained that I was a detective looking for a particular missing cat, they ascertained that I myself didn't own one and began the sales pitch all over again. One of them, after studying the photos, explained how I could take this geriatric, wildly overweight tabby home with me and apply a little dye to its left eyebrow and no one would know the difference.

It was dark when I got home, which means the cat had been missing for maybe thirty-one or thirty-two hours, which probably meant it had found a new home or lost a tussle with the kind of dog that could eat Marlowe for breakfast. At any rate, I was out of ideas and probably close to being out of work as well.

As a kid I'd dreamed of coming home to a loving wife, who'd rush to the door, throw her arms around me, and tell me how much she'd missed me, even though I'd only been gone for a few hours. When my marriage broke up, I occasionally daydreamed about coming home and being greeted by a loving dog that couldn't stop wagging his tail or jumping up and down from the sheer joy of being in my presence once again.

I opened the door and trudged in. Marlowe was sleeping on the couch. He opened one eye.

"I'm home," I announced.

He gave me a look that said, *Fine, just keep off my couch* and closed his eye again.

I took off the galoshes, kicked them into a closet, tossed the coat in after it, and went to the kitchen to pop open a Bud. That was when I discovered that we were out of beer. (I say "we" because I always put a little in a dish for Marlowe, who seemed to like it even better than I do.)

I turned on the TV, hoping that TCM was showing *All Through the Night* or one of my other favorite Bogey movies when there was a pounding at the door. My first thought was that it was Mrs. Pepperidge and she was firing me, but then I figured there was no way she could find my apartment, or that having found it she'd soil her hands by knocking at the door, so I got up, walked over, opened it, and found myself confronting Mrs. Cominsky, my landlady, who reminded me of Comiskey Park where the White Sox used to play, though she was even broader around the hips than the stadium was.

"What can I do you for?" I said.

"You're tracking slush and mud all through my foyer"—which she pronounced "foy-yay," though I'd swear she never made it past her sophomore year in high school—"and my staircase. I've warned you about this before, Mr. Paxton."

"So you have, Mrs. Cominsky," I said. "But until I learn to fly, I have to use the front entrance and the stairs."

She stared at me for a long moment. "So are you at least catching a gang of killers?"

"Actually, I'm trying to catch a cat."

"*In here?*" she bellowed. "You know my rules. I bent them for that mutt there"—she pointed at Marlowe, who opened his eyes when she yelled, curled his lip at her, and went right back to sleep—"but *no* cats."

"The cat's not here, Mrs. Cominsky," I explained.

"You're sure?" she said dubiously, looking around the living room.

"He's out *there* somewhere," I said, waving my arm in a gesture that took in half the continent.

"Cats are a dime a dozen," she said. "Someone's actually paying you to find one?"

I nodded. "Yeah."

"Damn," she said. "It's chilly standing out in the hallway here."

She looked at me expectantly. I tried to remember if I was up to date on the rent payments.

"Won't you come in?" I said.

"If you insist," she said, brushing by me.

I think she was still looking for the cat. Marlowe opened his eyes again, stared at her, growled a couple of times, and turned to me. *If she sits down on me*, his expression seemed to say, *I'm gonna give her a bite to remember.*

"When's the last time you vacuumed this carpet?" she said.

"It's not a carpet, it's a rug," I said. "And it's got more miles on it than my car."

"Stop avoiding the question."

I shrugged. "Been a long time, I guess."

"Maybe I'll do it for you," she said. "After all, it's really *my* carpet."

"Rug," I said.

"Whatever," she replied with a shrug of her own. "Where's your vacuum?"

"I left it in my other suit."

"You don't *have* another suit," she growled.

"I don't have a vacuum either."

"You know, Mr. Paxton . . ."

"Eli," I corrected her.

"Eli," she said. "I put up with a lot from you. Any given day you're late on the rent, you keep a mutt that acts as if the floor will gobble his feet if he ever gets off the furniture, and from what I read in the papers you're always getting shot at."

"Not always," I said. "Once, maybe twice a year." I paused. "Three times at most."

"And what am I going to do if you get killed while you're behind in the rent?"

"You'll inherit Marlowe," I said, who woke up at the sound of his name just enough to bare his teeth and then went back to sleep.

She sighed. "You're hopeless, Mr. Paxton. I like all my other tenants. They talk to me. They invite me in to visit. I don't feel as if I have to shower when I leave their apartments. They don't know all the crooks in town, and get shot at, and then have the temerity to tell me that someone's paying them to look for a cat, for God's sake."

"I'm sorry you feel that way," I said, vaguely wondering if there was a college football game on the TV.

"And the way you live!" she continued. "I'm not a knife, you know."

"A knife?" I repeated, frowning.

"You know—someone who doesn't know the score."

"I think you mean a *naïf*," I said.

"Whatever. Anyway, I read detective stories too. I know Lord Peter Wimsey doesn't live like this, and neither does Philo Vance."

"They're the new kids on the block," I said. "They work for higher fees."

She just stared at me for a long moment and finally said: "Get a life, Mr. Paxton! Get a life!"

I was going to tell her I'd love one and ask where they were selling them, but she'd walked back out and slammed the door behind her. Hell, I didn't even get a chance to remind her that Columbo was even more rumpled than I was.

Marlowe woke up when he heard the door and gave me a glare that said he wasn't leaving the couch and wasn't into sharing. I decided to go out for a snack and a beer, then remembered what the weather was like, went to the kitchen, opened a can of roast beef hash, decided I could live without the fried eggs that accompany it if it meant I didn't have to cook, and took a spoon and began eating it out of the can, which was probably the one thing in the universe that could get Marlowe to relinquish his couch, remind me that we were the Two Musketeers, and wait impatiently while I emptied a third of the can into his food bowl.

After we'd eaten, and both had to do without beer, we made our way back to the TV. ESPN was showing wrestling, poker, hockey, and high school football, and TCM had run through its store of old mystery series and was having a Bette Davis festival, so I wound up watching a bunch of steroid monsters hit each other with folding chairs and brag about who they were going to rassle (I never once heard any of them say "wrestle") next week, and finally Marlowe and I drifted off to sleep.

When I woke up they were showing woman's golf from somewhere on the far side of the world. I turned off the TV, considered heating up some coffee, decided that Marlowe looked decidedly restless, and figured I'd better take him for a walk before we gave Mrs. Cominsky something else to bitch about.

The weather was above freezing—it never stays cold for too long in Cincinnati—and that meant everything was melting, and five minutes later I brought a *very* wet dog back into the apartment.

I was drying him off with a towel, and he was showing me how very much he resented it, when the phone rang, so I walked over and picked it up.

"Mr. Paxton?" said a female voice.

"Yeah?" I replied.

"This is the Wilkinson Animal Shelter." Pause. "You were here yesterday, looking for a cat?"

"That's right."

"I believe we may have the one you were looking for," continued the voice. "Mackerel tabby, female, white spot above the left eye?"

"Sure as hell sounds like her," I said. "I'll be right over." Then I corrected myself. "Well, as soon as I can. You're about twenty, maybe thirty minutes north and west of me."

"She's not going anywhere."

I hung up the phone, left Marlowe sulking in a corner of the living room, and went down to my car. The roads were much more navigable, and even though the shelter was northwest of the city I made it in just over twenty minutes.

I pulled into their parking lot, was greeting by a chorus of barking from the runs in the back, and walked into the office.

"Hello, Mr. Paxton," said a gray-haired woman, the same one I'd seen the day before. "I believe we may be in luck, if you can identify the cat."

"I've never seen her in my life," I said. "Let's just see if she matches the photos."

"What name does she answer to?"

"Her name's Fluffy," I replied.

"I'll be right back," she said, walking into a room on the left side of the building. When she opened the door I heard maybe a dozen cats start meowing, and a moment later she emerged carrying a cat who seemed to be the one in the photos.

"It sure looks like her," I said.

"And you say she's from the east side of the city?"

I nodded. "The Grandin Road area, just south of Hyde Park—or maybe it's part of Hyde Park for all I know."

"It's very odd," she said. "You say she's been missing for two days?"

"Right."

"It's totally unheard of for a cat to come this far in such a short time."

"Maybe she hopped into the back of a truck for shelter," I suggested. "Or perhaps somebody picked her up, thought better of it, and turned her loose somewhere around here."

Her face said each was as unlikely as the other.

"What the hell," I said. "As long as we found her, it's not my job to worry about how she got here." I stared at the cat for a moment. "Let's *assume* it's her," I continued. "But if it's not ... ?"

"Then it means that she *is* local, and it would be best to bring her back here rather than dropping her off at Silverman's."

"Silverman's?" I asked.

"The closest shelter to the area she comes from."

"Okay," I said. "Do I have to pay you or sign something?"

She shook her head. "We're always happy to help the police, as well as return a loved pet to her home. Perhaps you'd like to make a donation?"

"I'll tell the grateful owner to," I replied quickly.

She reached beneath the counter and pulled out what looked like a cardboard box with windows and a handle. "You won't want her loose in the car while you're driving."

"The owner will take care of the donation," I repeated, "but I'll pay for the box."

"Five dollars," she said. "We don't make a profit on them."

I thanked her and paid her. Then she opened the box, put the cat in it and closed it, and a couple of minutes later I was on my way to the Pepperidge house. The cat yowled continuously, and I got the distinct impression that she was objecting to my car or my driving or both.

But none of her yowls could depress me. I was too busy doing my math: fifteen hundred in the kick, four hundred for two days' work (or maybe six hundred if getting the cat in the morning counted as a day), and a thousand-dollar bonus for finding her. That would take care of the transmission, pay a couple of months' rent, and maybe even buy a small display ad in the yellow pages.

I was feeling pretty good when I pulled into the Pepperidge driveway, climbed out of the car, grabbed the box by its handle, and walked up to the front door. There was only one cop car still there, and a uniformed cop opened the door before I could ring the buzzer.

"Get the boss lady down here," I said. "I've got her cat."

He ushered me into the kitchen, where I couldn't drip on any wildly expensive carpeting, told me to wait there, and went off to get Mrs. Pepperidge. I put the crate on a granite counter and waited.

She rushed into the kitchen half a minute later.

"Here she is, Mrs. Pepperidge," I said, opening the box and letting the cat step out to the counter. "Your adorable Fluffy."

She frowned and stepped forward.

"Where is it?" she demanded harshly.

"It's right here," I said, indicating the cat.

She swiped her arm across the counter, knocking the cat, which uttered a surprised yowl, to the floor.

"Where *is* it?" she said again.

"Isn't that your cat?" I asked, not totally disappointed since it meant I was still on salary.

"Of course it's my cat!"

"Then—?" I began.

"Where's the goddamned collar?"

"Ma'am, the cat wasn't wearing any collar."

She glared at me for a long minute, then turned to the cop.

"Officer, arrest this man."

"For what, ma'am?" asked the surprised cop.

"Theft."

"But he returned your cat," said the cop. "If that's not her—"

"Just arrest the son of a bitch!" she screamed.

"But—"

"I am not without influence in this town," she bellowed. "If I have to go to your superiors, it'll go as hard with you as with this thieving bastard here."

"Let me just check with headquarters, Mrs. Pepperidge, ma'am," said the cop, pulling out his cell phone.

And forty seconds later I was taken into custody, given my very own cell in the Cincinnati jail, and charged with a felony.

4.

Some sadist built the huge, glitzy, noisy Horseshoe Casino right across street from the jail, so just about every cell had a clear view of it. You could sit on your cot—I hesitate to call it a *bed*—and look out at all the high rollers, as well as the chronic losers, wandering in all day long, and if you were in for touting or picking pockets you practically went nuts seeing your rivals home in on all that easy money.

I'd been cooling my heels there for maybe six hours, idly wondering which of my clothes Marlowe would eat first when his food dish remained empty, when a guard turned his key in the lock and Jim Simmons entered the cell.

"Eli, what the hell is going on?" he asked. "I just heard about this."

"Beats the hell out of me," I answered.

"What the hell was so important about the cat's collar?"

I shrugged. "I have no idea," I told him. "I never saw it."

"You didn't steal it?"

"I came right to the Pepperidge house from the shelter, or whatever the hell you call it. They've already searched me, and I'm sure they searched my car before we even reached the jail."

"All right," he said. "I'm letting you out of here."

"The lady's got friends in high places," I warned him.

"This isn't goddamned New York or Chicago!" he growled. "Nobody tells me I can't let an innocent man go free."

"I think she'd argue that I'm not an innocent man."

"She's got a funeral to attend tomorrow. Just don't turn up at it," said Simmons. "Now get up and we'll get you the hell out of here."

"When did you become a Samaritan?" I asked.

"When I realized that if I hadn't recommended you for the job you'd still be free."

"And broke," I added. "So thanks for that much."

As we reached the ground floor he looked out. "It'll be dark in ten minutes," he said. "Let's stop at the Twenty Yard Line for a beer, and then I'll drive you to your car. No one will stop us or even see who it is in the dark—and if you had so much as a dirty photo of some blonde teenager in the car it would have been reported already."

So we walked to the Twenty Yard Line, sat at a polished bar that had oversized photos of Ken Anderson, Boomer Esiason, Carson Palmer, and Andy Dalton staring down at us, discussed the Super Bowl for a minute or two, but since we didn't think the Bengals could get there and we didn't want to get thrown out on our asses for saying so, we changed the subject and fell to predicting the likely Derby prospects for next spring.

We finished our beers, Jim drove me to the Pepperidge house—and did the last half-block with his headlights off—I climbed out of the car and walked three feet to my own, spent a few minutes trying to wake up the gremlin in the ignition, and finally got it going and drove off before anyone from inside the house paid any attention.

"Well, so it's Kojak, home from another case," said Mrs. Cominsky, who was standing in the foyer with folded arms.

"Kojak was public, I'm private," I told her. "Also, Kojak was imaginary. I'm real."

"So's your dog."

I turned to her. "Oh?"

"When I realized you'd been gone all day, I went upstairs to feed the poor ugly creature. I think he's dying."

"He was fine when I left," I said, frowning.

"I fed him a can of Alpo, which is just about the best dog food on the market, and he was too weak to get off the couch and eat it."

I relaxed. "He could smell it from the couch." She stared at me, and I smiled. "He doesn't eat dog food."

It was her turn to frown. "What *does* he eat?"

I shrugged. "Pizza. Hamburgers. Cheese Danishes. Peanut butter and jelly sandwiches. Whatever I'm having."

"I don't know why I put up with either of you!" she snapped and went back inside.

I checked the mail—no bills for a change, but no *Playboy* or *Hustler* either, which meant the day was a wash. I went upstairs, opened the door, told Marlowe to stop snoring and get ready for a walk, attached the leash to his collar, and a moment later we were walking through the mud and slush. Sometimes Cincinnati gets a foot of snow, usually just an inch, but whichever it gets, it always warms up fast and melts everything just as fast. Marlowe and I figured that Mrs. Garabaldi's petunias had missed him, so he went over to renew old acquaintances, and I got to hear her cursing at us in Italian, as usual.

Then we began walking back to the apartment, and as we did so I became aware of the fact that one of us, either Marlowe or me, was being watched. There was a guy in a parked car—I couldn't make out his features in the dark—and he was staring at us intently. I'd had enough hassles for one day, so I just kept on walking, with Marlowe absolutely determined not to walk at my side but pulling me forward until we finally made it home. I half-expected Mrs. Cominsky to be waiting with another lecture, but she was in her living room watching wealthy, well-connected detectives on TV, and Marlowe and I made it to the apartment unmolested.

I opened the door, and Marlowe made a beeline for the couch just in case I had any foolish thoughts of sitting on it, so I wandered into the kitchen to see what there was to eat, since they'd forgotten to feed me lunch at the jail and I'd been too annoyed to ask. I opened the fridge, found a package of hot dogs, decided cooking just made them warmer, not better, pulled the pack out, walked back into the living room, turned on the TV, and sat down on the couch next to Marlowe.

"Dinner," I said, offering him a hot dog. He took it and decided I could stay on the couch without his lying on his side and digging his feet into me, and I flipped through about fifteen channels on the remote. There were a ton of news shows with all the usual—everyone hated us, the economy was in the tank, terrorists wanted to blow up New York or maybe Los Angeles, which at least meant I wouldn't have to hear the network commentators sing their love songs about the Yankees and the Lakers, a couple of hurricanes were racing neck-and-neck to see which could destroy the Gulf Coast first. And finally they came to the only important news of the day: Carlos Dunlap's ankle had responded to treatment, and he was a probable when the Bengals hosted the Steelers on Sunday.

I turned back to TCM. At least they were done with Bette Davis and Joan Crawford. The problem was that Bettie Page had never made a film that lasted much more than ten or twelve minutes, so they were having a Veronica Lake festival. I turned it off, picked up an old paperback about a brilliant detective who never lost a fight and couldn't have kept the gorgeous, oversexed women away with a gallon of mace. I fell asleep somewhere in chapter three and woke up to find that it was morning, Marlowe had eaten the rest of the hot dogs, and had wiped his mouth off on my now-incredibly-damp paperback.

I considered showering, but I didn't want to get out of my clothes only to climb right back in them five minutes later, so I settled for a quick shave and a cup of coffee, and then Marlowe and I visited Mrs. Garabaldi's petunias again, but she was either asleep or out and there was no ear-shattering cursing, and I could tell Marlowe kind of missed it.

Then I put him back in the house, got into the car, and drove off to the Wilkinson Animal Shelter.

"Good morning, Officer Paxton," said the lady behind the desk. "How may I help you today?"

"It's just plain Eli, ma'am," I said.

She gave me a knowing look that said, *Ah! You're working under-cover. Okay, you can trust me to keep your secret.*

"All right, Eli. And my name is Susan. What can I do for you?"

"The cat I picked up yesterday . . ." I began.

"Yes?" said Susan. "I believe you said her name was Fluffy."

"That's correct."

"Wasn't she the right cat?"

"She was the right cat."

"Good!" Suddenly Susan frowned. "Then what are you doing back here?"

"Just checking some details," I said. "Did she have a collar when she was brought in?"

"No," she replied. "If she had, we'd have kept it on her. And if it had a license tag, we'd have known to phone the owner."

"I was afraid you were going to say that," I said.

"Can you describe it?"

I shook my head. "I have no idea what it looks like. It wasn't in any of the photos I had."

"Then why—?"

"The owner wants it back."

Susan nodded knowingly. "A sentimental keepsake from a previous cat, no doubt."

I decided to reach for my only other possible lead. "Did the cat wander in on her own, or did someone bring her in?"

"She was brought in by a gentleman," was the answer.

"Did he leave his name?"

Susan shook her head. "No. He said he found her wandering on the street a few blocks away. His heart went out to her, and he picked her up and put her in his car. Evidently, he has a couple of large dogs, and he didn't think the cat would be safe at home. I asked for his name and address, but he insisted he was just performing an act of Christian charity and didn't want the owner calling to thank him." She smiled. "I think his real reason was that he didn't want us calling him for donations."

If the collar was enough reason to get me charged with theft and thrown into jail, I could think of a different reason he didn't want to leave his name, but there was no sense discussing it with her. I couldn't even tell her to keep an eye out for the collar, since I didn't know what it looked like.

"Well, thank you anyway, Susan," I said. "Just trying to be thorough."

"I'm glad it was the right cat," she replied. "And I'm sure you're anxious to go back to apprehending killers and bank robbers and the like."

"It's what I live for," I assured her, and returned to my car.

I got hungry on the way back—which made sense; all I'd had since yesterday morning was a pair of uncooked hot dogs, without even buns—so I stopped by a Bob Evans, sat down at a booth, and ordered a cup of coffee and a breakfast of steak and eggs without bothering to read the menu, since it was the same in all ten thousand Bob Evans restaurants, or however many there were in the Cincinnati area.

The waitress—I haven't gotten around to calling them "servers" yet—brought the coffee, and as I was adding a little cream, just to bring out the subtle nuances of the flavor, a short, burly, well-muscled man with a thick shock of coal-black hair and a matching black mustache sat down across from me.

"We should talk, Mr. Paxton," he said.

"You've been watching me and following me since I got out of jail, and you've decided based on that that I'm a sterling conversationalist?" I said.

He grinned. "You're as good as they say you are, Mr. Paxton."

"Thank them for me."

"Maybe we can do some business and you can thank them yourself, Mr. Paxton."

"Call me Eli. And who do I have the honor of speaking to?"

"Val Sorrentino," he said, extending his hand. "From Chicago."

"Not Cicero?" I said, taking his hand.

"Well, I go home at night."

"Why have you sought me out, Val Sorrentino?" I asked.

"Because you're working for Velma Palanto," he said.

"If she's who I think she is, she fired me and had me arrested yesterday morning."

"Hah! I *knew* it!" Suddenly he grinned at me. "That's why we can do some business together—because you're *not* working for her."

"I'm not working for Warren Buffett either," I said. "How much is *that* worth?"

He threw back his head and laughed. "I *like* you, Eli!" he said. "We're gonna get along fine together."

"Excuse me for asking," I said, "but what do you think we're going to be doing while we're getting along fine together?"

He looked around to make sure no one was listening.

"I belong to a certain family that I suspect you're not unfamiliar with, since you spent some time on the Chicago Police Force a while back."

"It's possible," I replied.

"Anyway, this family employed a financial wizard named James Palanto. Big Jim, we called him."

"I believe I've heard the name in the last couple of days," I said.

"A few members of my family . . . ," he began carefully.

"Distant cousins, no doubt," I said.

He smiled. "Absolutely. No one I ever met personally, of course."

"Of course," I agreed.

"Anyway, these distant cousins have been unfairly charged with committing a series of . . . well, boyish pranks."

Like murder, drug dealing, and extortion, I thought, but I managed not to say anything.

"And while Big Jim Palanto set off on his own with the family's blessing quite a few years ago, word has reached them that these totally corrupt accusers . . ."

The Chicago cops, I thought.

". . . planned to subpoena him and get him to testify against them, who of course Palanto loved like brothers."

I frowned. "If you came here to make sure he didn't testify, why are you wasting time talking to me? Why aren't you back in Chicago?"

"You cut me to the quick, Mr. Paxton," he said.

"Eli," I corrected him.

"I didn't off him," he continued, forgetting to be circumspect. "I was here to sound him out, and he convinced me he wasn't going to implicate nobody for nothing."

"So you didn't put him out of the misery of pretending to be law-abiding Malcolm Pepperidge?"

"Perish the thought," replied Sorrentino. "I spoke to him a few days ago, and everything was copacetic."

"Then why are you still in town?" I asked, puzzled.

He shot me his biggest grin of all. "Because I couldn't see no reason why you and I shouldn't make a quick ten million dollars."

5.

For just a minute I thought I was going to choke on my coffee.

"Calm down, Mr. Paxton," said Sorrentino with an amused smile. "You look like you're about to have a stroke."

I got the coffee down and wiped my mouth off with my sleeve.

"You shouldn't tell jokes like that when there's food or drink on the table," I said.

His smile vanished. "I'm not joking."

"Ten million?" I said, and he nodded his head. "Okay, you're not joking—you're delusional."

"You wanna hear me out, or you wanna make cute remarks?"

I stared at him. He didn't *look* like a raving lunatic. But talking eight digits to a guy who couldn't afford a new transmission for his twelve-year-old car wasn't the mark of a man who was on the level and playing with all his marbles.

"Well?" he said.

"I suppose it's just good manners to hear you out," I replied. "Ten million, you say?"

He shrugged. "It's a ballpark figure. Could be as low as eight million, could be as high as twelve or thirteen."

"Whose is it?"

"Right at the moment, probably nobody's," answered Sorrentino.

"Maybe you'd better begin at the beginning," I suggested, as the waitress arrived with my steak and eggs.

"Just coffee for me, Toots," said Sorrentino. I was almost surprised that the glare she gave him didn't knock him over. "What do you know about Big Jim?"

"I never heard of him until two days ago," I said. "Under *either* of his names."

"He was a straight shooter," said Sorrentino, "and a really good guy. A hell of a lot nicer than that bitch he married, that Velma, though she was quite a looker twenty years ago. Anyway, Big Jim was as honest as the day is long."

"I thought he worked for the mob."

"So let me qualify that. He was loyal to his employers, never stole or misplaced a nickel, and would have gone into stir before he ratted them out, though of course it never came to that."

"Okay, he was one of Nature's noblemen," I said.

"Absolutely," said Sorrentino with something akin to passion. "You couldn't ask for a straighter shooter."

"He shot people?"

"Figure of speech," he added. "Anyway, the man was a financial genius. And then one day he just walked away from it. Turned over all the books and all the money to my bosses, said he'd had enough, that he didn't feel like a criminal but rather an accountant and financial advisor. He didn't think the cops or the feds would see it that way, and he wanted to get out while the getting was good."

"And they let him go?"

"He'd tripled their money, and this was how they showed their gratitude."

"That's better than some New York families I've heard about."

"So he sold his place up in Lake Forest, changed his name legally, and he and Velma just vanished. My bosses spent a year tracking him down, just in case they ever needed him again, but they never made contact with him. In fact, he couldn't believe his eyes when I showed up."

"So you showed up, he convinced you he wasn't turning state's evidence . . ."

". . . and that was that," concluded Sorrentino.

"But it *wasn't*," I pointed out. "You're still here."

"One moment," he said as the waitress returned with a fresh pot of coffee and a cup. "You got a cheese Danish back there in the kitchen, honey?"

"This is Bob Evans," she said harshly. "Read the menu." She began walking away, then stopped and turned. "And my name is Matilda."

"Figures," said Sorrentino as she vanished into the kitchen. He took a sip of his coffee. "Damned good stuff," he said approvingly. "What the hell have they got to go with it?"

I shoved the menu across to him. He read it quickly, then signaled a man who was cleaning a nearby table. "Hey, kid, bring me a sweet roll. Any kind you got, as long as it's got frosting on it."

The man, who was in his midthirties, nodded and went off without a word.

"You were saying?" I began.

"About cheese Danish?" he replied. "Nothing goes better with a cup of coffee before noon."

"About Big Jim Palanto."

"Poor bastard."

"And why you're still here?"

He nodded, then placed a forefinger to his lips as Matilda arrived with his sweet roll, glared at him, and walked off.

"Big Jim had a talent, and so did that bitch he married," said Sorrentino. "His was making money, hers was spending it."

"Sounds like my former marriage," I said. "Except for the making money part."

"Well, about eight or ten years ago he decided he needed a serious source of income, so he went back into the same business. Not for my employers, of course. They'd long since replaced him."

I frowned. "I don't know quite where this is leading," I said, "but Cincinnati doesn't *have* a mob."

"Look south."

"South is Kentucky," I replied. "South that makes sense is Mexico."

"*Farther* south."

I just stared at him.

"Bolivia," he said at last.

"Okay, Bolivia," I said. "So what?"

"They saw what Colombia and Mexico were making from drugs, and they went into the business themselves. Now, Big Jim had nothing to do with the marketing, or any of the rough stuff that went along with it, but he made his expertise available to the Bolivians."

"He invested their drug money," I said.

"Right."

"If he was as good as you say, they should be happy as clams," I said. Not that I've ever seen a happy clam, or even a live one.

"Well, it appears that Big Jim decided he was getting up in years, and that he wanted to feather his nest a little faster than certain parties were happy about."

I just stared at him for a moment. "He *stole* from South American drug lords?"

"I'm sure he didn't look at it that way," answered Sorrentino. "As near as we can tell, he made them about fifty million dollars." He paused. "Problem is, he only gave them maybe forty million of it."

"So you think *they* killed him?"

"He was the salt of the earth, and he parted clean and fair with my employers," said Sorrentino. "Who else would have done it?"

"Oh, come on," I said. "How about anybody who knew he was loaded and thought they could pull off a robbery?"

"Nothing was missing," answered Sorrentino. Then he gave me a huge grin. "Well, *almost* nothing."

I stared at him, considered what I'd heard, then thought back to the little scene with the grieving widow in the Pepperidge house that resulted in my being jailed, and suddenly it became clear as crystal.

"Shit!" I said so loud that diners from two and three tables away turned to stare—and frown—at me.

He grinned again. "You got it."

"The collar!" I exclaimed.

He nodded. "The collar."

"What makes a collar worth ten million dollars?"

"Maybe only eight million," he corrected me.

"Yeah, I know," I replied. "And maybe twelve million. What makes it worth more than a buck and a half?"

"When I went to visit him—Velma was off shopping, which is her main occupation these days—he assured me he wasn't going to rat on his friends. We got to talking, he mentioned that he'd been doing some work for the Bolivians, and had given himself a raise in pay, and was trying to extricate himself from the unhappy situation. I told him that from what I'd heard, these South Americans had absolutely no respect for law and order, and that they might be after him even as we spoke. He told me that at least they'd never get their hands on the money, that he didn't have a safe, and that if Velma saw more than fifteen or twenty large in the checking account she immediately went out and spent it."

"I hope you're not going to tell me he had CDs glued to the inside of the collar," I said.

He chuckled. "No, I'm not going to tell you that." He reached into a coat pocket. "Here," he said, withdrawing a leather cat collar studded with what looked like ten or twelve gleaming diamonds. "What do you think of this?"

"Is *that* the collar?"

"Not quite," he replied with a smile. He pressed it against a water glass and began rubbing it against the surface. Nothing happened.

"Rhinestones," he explained. "Diamonds would have cut through it, or at least left some deep marks. I paid twenty bucks for it this morning. The collar we're talking about looks pretty much like this one. The only difference is that the stones were twenty-carat diamonds, and they'd have cut the glass."

"He admitted it?"

Sorrentino grinned. "He said the Bolivians would never think to look at a housecat's collar, and then he laughed his head off."

"Well, *someone* thought of it," I said. "Mrs. Pepperidge had me arrested and jailed when I returned the cat without the collar."

He uttered an amused laugh. "Hah! Big Jim didn't think she knew. That Velma can sniff out money from three states away, let alone half a room."

"But *she* doesn't have the collar," I pointed out. "That's what I was being paid to find, though I didn't know it at the time." I paused for a moment, thinking it through. "So the Bolivians must have figured it out, grabbed the collar, and either tossed the cat off the balcony into the snow, or closed the sliding door and locked him outside, after which he jumped."

Sorrentino shook his head. "Uh-uh."

"Why not?"

"They're still in town, three of them—and they took a shot at me last night. Someone else has the collar."

"Who?"

He shrugged. "Could be someone else knew about it. Could be someone saw it on the cat when it was locked outside and figured out what it was worth. Could be some kid fell in love with the cat, brought it inside, his mama said no, and he kept the collar as a keepsake. You're a detective; that's why I'm telling you this, and that's why we're gonna be partners."

I stared at him for a long minute, then finally shook my head, "I don't think so," I said.

"Why the hell not?"

"I don't want a bunch of Bolivian killers after me if we find it—and if we do find it, they'll know it the instant I catch up on my bills and you go back to Chicago."

"So you're just gonna leave it for *them* to find?"

"No, I'll search for it."

He frowned. "Half isn't enough for you?"

"Calm down," I said. "Ten percent is enough for me."

"What are you talking about?"

"I don't want any part of hot diamonds, either unloading them on the black market or keeping one step ahead of the Bolivians," I said. "But they have to be insured. If I find them, I'll turn them over to the insurance company for the standard finder's fee. We'll see that word gets out, and they can go home or rob the insurance company."

He glared at me. "*Half* a finder's fee," he said. "Remember, I'm the one who told you about them."

"You're going to be looking too?" I asked.

"You bet your ass I am," he assured me. "Why do you think I haven't gone back to Chicago? After all, Big Jim's not in a position to rat on anybody."

"So are we partners or competitors?" I asked.

He stared at me for a long time, then shrugged and extended his hand. "Partners."

"Okay," I said, taking his hand and shaking it. "If the Bolivians are still here, we know *they* haven't got them."

"Ain't much to go on," he said.

"Oh, we know a little more than that."

He looked surprised. "We do?"

I nodded. "We know they're not in the Grandin Road area."

"Why the hell not?"

"There are five animal shelters closer to the Pepperidge house than the one the cat turned up at. Believe me, I've been to all of them. Maybe whoever stole the cat and the collar didn't want it showing up a few blocks away, where someone might recognize a car or a driver, or at least be able to identify them—but no one drove twenty-five miles through that blizzard just to dump the cat where nobody knew it or them—and no pampered housecat walks twenty-five miles in two days in this weather."

"They said you were good," he replied approvingly. "Okay, we'll keep in touch three or four times a day. What's your cell number?"

"I don't have one."

He looked hurt. "I thought we were partners."

"We are," I replied. "I just don't have a cell phone."

He frowned. "I suppose a tablet that lets you answer any e-mails I send to you is out of the question?"

I nodded. "Afraid so."

He sighed deeply. "Do you at least carry a gun?"

"Almost never."

"I know you solved a murder down in Kentucky last year and exposed a major drug ring before that." He stared curiously at me. "Just what century do you operate in?"

I shrugged. "I think I'd have been really effective working for Tom Jefferson."

He half-nodded in agreement. "At least if you worked for old Tom you wouldn't have three Bolivian hit men with maybe twenty kills between them racing you for the collar and ready to blow you away if you find it first." He pulled out a pen and wrote on a napkin. "This is *my* cell number. Check in two or three times a day." I was about to answer when he held up his hand. "No more bullshit. Use a pay phone."

"Right," I said, vaguely wondering what pay phones cost these days. "Where will you go first?"

"I don't know . . . but it makes the most sense for *you* to find out about the Bolivians. After all, this is your town. You've got to have some snitches who can tell you what's going on."

I was happy to hear him use the word "snitches." It was comforting to know *something* I was familiar with hadn't vanished before the turn of the century. "I'll see what I can find out," I told him.

"I'll check with my people and see which fences out of the Cincinnati area can handle that kind of hot material. Where should we meet for dinner?"

"What do you like?" I asked.

"Diamonds," he said.

"What else?"

"If it's smaller than me, I'll eat it," said Sorrentino.

It was comforting to know that I'd picked up a partner with the same taste.

6.

I figured the first thing I'd better do was contact Jim Simmons. I didn't want to do it in front of any other cops, so I phoned him at his office and told him to meet me at the usual place, and sure enough he showed up twenty minutes later at Red's Jungle, the bar we'd meet at before or after a game. The owner was a very nice gray-haired lady whose name wasn't Red, and the field hadn't been The Jungle since Boomer Esiason took the Bengals to the Super Bowl back in 1989, but it had the right atmosphere: if you were going to or coming from a baseball or football game, this was the place to be.

Jim was in a corner booth when I got there, and I walked over and sat down opposite him.

"I figured whatever you had to say, you didn't want to say it at the bar where anyone could overhear," he said by way of greeting.

"Right," I answered.

"So is this about the cat—or hopefully about the deceased?" he asked. "Or are you on a new case?"

"Same case," I said. "Though I'm freelancing now. I have a feeling that Velma—Mrs. Pepperidge—doesn't want to hire me back."

He grinned at that. "Okay, what is it that you want to share with me?"

I learned forward. "Jim, I figure someone in the department should know that there are three Bolivian hitters involved somehow, and they're in town."

He looked at me in disbelief. "Bolivian?" he repeated, half-smiling. "Not Paraguayan or Ecuadorian?"

I waited for Red to come by and take our drinks order and then answered him. "It's complicated. But they *are* Bolivian, they *are* killers, they may have killed Pepperidge, and they're still in town."

He pulled out a notebook and a pen. "Names?"

"I don't know."

"Okay, descriptions?"

"I don't know."

"How much have you had to drink, Eli?" he asked.

"Not a drop until Red gets back with my beer."

He shook his head. "This isn't like you. You're holding back something, probably a bunch of somethings. I can't act on what little you've told me."

"Okay," I said. "What I told you is for public consumption. What I'm going to say next is for you alone. If you *have* to pass parts of it along to save a life, of course you have to. But otherwise it's for your ears only until I tell you otherwise."

"Fair enough," he said as Red brought my beer and Jim's bourbon to the table.

"Some weather we're having," she said. "And the poor bastards are playing at home this weekend. You think they'll *ever* put a dome on the damned stadium?"

"Not a chance," said Simmons. "Same reason they don't dome Soldier Field in Chicago or Lambeau Field in Green Bay. We're used to cold weather. Those warm-weather teams from Florida and California aren't, so this gives us an advantage. Remember the Ice Bowl? Anthony Muñoz and the guys came out in their short-sleeved jerseys, the San Diego Chargers took one look at them, and for all practical purposes the game was over before it started."

"I'm way too young to remember that," lied Red.

"Of course you are," lied Simmons. "My mistake."

She kissed him on his bald spot and want back to the bar.

"You're quite a ladies' man," I said with a smile.

"Old ladies," he answered. "The young ones see right through me." He paused. "Okay, what have you learned that I can't tell to anyone else unless the Iranians—excuse me: the Bolivians—bomb the city."

"You know anything more about Palanto than what you told me?"

"Just what we have in the files," he answered. "Hell, you can probably find it on *Wikipedia*."

"Whatever *that* is."

He rolled his eyes and shook his head sadly. "I'll never understand why you don't ride a horse and carry a six-gun." Then: "Yes, that's pretty much all I know about Palanto. Clearly you're about to tell me more."

"He didn't exactly retire when he moved here and became Malcolm Pepperidge," I said.

Simmons looked surprised. "He kept working for the mob in Chicago? Now, *that's* interesting."

I shook my head. "He kept his word and never worked for them again. But either he missed the work or he missed the rewards, because he began doing the same thing for a Bolivian drug cartel."

He stared long and hard at me. "Okay, I give up. Who told you?"

"Ever hear of Val Sorrentino?" I said.

"You're traveling in rough company, Eli. He's one of the mob's enforcers." He frowned. "What the hell's *he* doing in town?" The frown vanished. "Of course! The mob sent him here to make sure Palanto couldn't testify!"

"Now that you've solved the murder, do you want to hear what I know or not?" I said.

"Shoot," he said, and then added: "You should pardon the expression."

"Sorrentino was sent here by his bosses to sound Palanto out, to see if he was going to testify. He told them a day or two before the murder that Palanto was safe and dependable, that they had nothing to worry about."

Simmons stared at me. "You believe that?"

"I do."

He took a deep breath, then pushed it out so that his lips vibrated. He sounded like a horse that just came back after a hard six furlongs. "You're too good a cop—"

"Detective," I interrupted him.

"You're too good at either to believe it based just on what you told me. What else should I know?"

"This is confidential, right?" I said.

He nodded his head. "Right."

"Jim, the word I get is that he held back ten million dollars from the Bolivians. They're in town to get it back."

"So *they* killed him?"

I shrugged. "I don't know. I don't even know if they had a reason to."

Simmons frowned again. "Then he *didn't* steal ten million?"

"I'm assuming he did."

He looked totally confused. "Then they *did* have a reason to off him."

"They had a reason to be here," I said. "They had a reason to want their millions back if Sorrentino is correct about how much Palanto siphoned off. But until they knew where he hid the money, they had every reason to keep him alive and absolutely no reason to kill him."

"Something's missing here," said Simmons. "Maybe they knew where the money was and then killed him and grabbed it—or grabbed it and killed him."

I shook my head. "Not a chance."

"Okay, why not?" he asked.

"They're still in town, and that means they *don't* know where the money is."

Simmons stared at me for a long moment. "But *you* know," he said at last.

"I know where at least some of it is," I said.

"Well?" he demanded.

"It's why Velma—Mrs. Pepperidge—paid me a hundred times what the cat was worth to find it and had me arrested when I brought it back without its collar."

He looked disbelievingly at me. "What was the fucking thing made of?"

"Leather. But it was studded with what looked like rhinestones, but which according to Sorrentino were actually diamonds—and that's why I know that whoever killed him didn't know what the collar was worth. Whether it was the Bolivians or someone else, why not just shoot the cat too, and remove the collar?"

"So you think that's why the Bolivians are still in town?" asked Simmons.

"Can you think of any other reason?" I shot back.

"And I assume Sorrentino is still around too?"

I nodded. "We've formed a kind of partnership."

"Oh?"

"If we find the collar, we turn it in for the reward."

"*Is* there one?" asked Simmons. "I haven't heard anything about it."

"If it's insured, we'll collect from the insurance company. And whether it is or not, Velma will offer a hefty reward for it. Probably under a phony name so anyone who's watching her to see if she can recover it doesn't dope it out. I figure if she gets it, the first few thousand go to a facelift and a new name, the next few for plane fare, and good luck ever finding her again."

"So did *she* do it, maybe?"

"Doesn't seem likely, though of course you'll check her bridge alibi. She had access to that cat day in and day out. Why the hell let it run off in a snowstorm with the collar still on?"

"It sneaked out?" Simmons suggested, but even he didn't look like he believed it.

"All she had to do was take the collar off before she shot him, Jim," I said. "Then let the cat go or stay, and who would know or care?"

"Okay," he said. "So Palanto was killed by Velma or three mysterious Bolivian shooters of which we have no record—there aren't any international flights to Cincinnati from anywhere except France and Canada. Or maybe it was your pal Sorrentino." He paused. "Or servants?" he suggested unenthusiastically.

I shook my head. "If they knew about the collar, why not just take it and run? Why commit murder?"

He nodded his agreement. "You got a point." He smiled. "I just hate it when you got a point." He checked his watch. "Any other possibilities?"

"Yeah," I said. "The guy who turned the cat in to the shelter without its collar."

He looked interested. "You know who it was?"

I shook my head. "Not yet."

"Surely they have a record."

"He didn't give his name."

Simmons grimaced. "So that's it?"

"So far," I replied "I'll keep you informed of anything I learn."

"And I'll let you know if the collar turns up." He finished his drink and stood up. "I hate to kiss and run, but I have to see what we have on any recent arrivals from—" he shook his head in wonderment "—Bolivia." He began putting on his heavy winter overcoat. "And you got quite a few leads to follow up: Bolivians, widows, mob enforcers . . ."

I smiled. "Not *me*, Jim. Murder is *your* business. I'm just looking for a cat collar. And since I suspect my partner isn't as interested in turning it in for the reward as I am, my only problem is finding it before he does."

But of course I was wrong.

7.

I drove home, checking the rearview mirror every few seconds to see if I was being followed, but there were so damned many cars on the road it was impossible to tell. When I got to my street I went once around the block, just to make sure. Then I parked, entered the building, and climbed up the stairs to my apartment.

Mrs. Cominsky was waiting for me.

"Where the hell have you been?" she half-asked and half-demanded.

"Out," I said. "And if you ask what did I do, the answer is nothing. But it's nice to know you care."

"I care about all my tenants," she said. Then: "You had a visitor. Well, a caller, I suppose you'd say. Hard to be a visitor if no one is there to let you in."

I wanted to say, "Electric or phone?" but on the off-chance it wasn't a bill collector I waited for her to tell me.

"Spoke with a real accent," she continued.

"Bolivian?" I asked.

"Bolivian?" she repeated. "Isn't that the wristwatch?"

"Did he say who he was?"

"No, just that he had some business with you."

"Did he have a couple of friends with him, or maybe waiting in his car?"

"How would I know which his car was?" she replied. "And he was alone."

"No message?"

She shook her head.

"Okay, thanks," I said, starting to climb the stairs again.

"I'm a landlady, not a message desk," she said as I reached my door.

I put the key in the lock, turned it, and entered. Marlowe was snoring on the couch. He opened one eye, stared blearily at me, and went back to sleep.

"I wish just once you'd run up and greet me with tail a-wag when I walk into the place," I said.

I wish just once you'd remember your job is to feed me and let me sleep twenty-two hours a day, he seemed to reply.

I thought maybe I'd open the mail, but I remembered that I hadn't picked it up yet. Finally I decided Marlowe looked too damned smug and comfortable, so I put the leash on him and walked him down the street where he watered Mrs. Garabaldi's petunias, and the fact that they were dead didn't stop her from opening her window and treating the neighborhood to some Italian words they never heard in a spaghetti Western.

I took Marlowe back home, opened a can of baked beans for him, and left the apartment while he was busy alternating between mouthfuls of food and growls at unseen rivals. I remembered to check the mailbox on the way out, found that I had only one letter—a reminder from my dentist that I hadn't seen him in three years—and climbed into my car.

I drove downtown, parked illegally since I knew I could count on Jim Simmons to fix any parking tickets, and walked to the edge of the rundown Over-the-Rhine area a bit more than a mile away. I attracted a few stares and a couple of panhandlers and a forty-ish hooker, but nothing out of the ordinary for the vicinity. Then I reached Ziggy's Cut-Rate Tailor Shop with his Lincoln parked out front and walked in.

Ziggy, all five foot two inches of him, was sitting on a chair behind the counter, reading the *Racing Form.* The same half-dozen pairs of trousers that had been there for the last ten years were on hangers, attached to the wall behind him.

"Hi, Eli," he said, looking up from the *Form.*

"You ought to change those pants, Ziggy," I said. "No one wears cuffs anymore. Someone might get the idea that you're a fence who just uses the tailor business as a front."

"Hah! That's all *you* know!" he shot back. "Cuffs are making a comeback."

"Why?" I asked. "The only thing they were good for was stashing your cigarette butts until you could dump 'em outside, and no one smokes anymore."

"You do."

"Well, hardly anyone."

"We gonna trade pleasantries all day, or are you gonna tell me why you're here? I'll be happy to sell you a suit while we wait."

I shook my head. "No, it's business."

"Isn't it always?" he said. "Okay, what are you after?"

"I don't think anyone's had a chance yet to bring in what I'm looking for yet, but I want to warn you."

He frowned. "*Warn* me?"

"Yeah. There are going to be some very big, very hot, very dangerous diamonds on the market pretty soon."

"How big?"

"I haven't seen them," I said. "What if I told you they might retail for ten million?"

His eyes widened. "Ten *million?*" he repeated. "Not ten thousand?"

"Could be seven or eight million, could be eleven or twelve. Ten's a ballpark figure."

"That's some ballpark!" he said and uttered a low whistle. Then he frowned. "Are you *sure*? Because no one in Cincinnati is sitting on ten million worth of diamonds. If they were, I'd have heard about it."

"There are reasons why no one knows," I said.

"Okay," he said. "For the moment I'll pretend we're talking ten million bucks. How many hundreds of diamonds are we looking for?"

I pointed to his leather watchband. "They'd all fit on *that*," I said.

He frowned. "Do you know what you're saying, Eli? You're talking maybe ten diamonds the size of, I dunno, golf balls."

I shook my head. "They couldn't be."

"I'm telling you . . ."

I didn't want to say that they'd be too obvious on the collar, or even that a cat was carrying them around. I already had one criminal helping me look for them; I didn't need another.

"How about something the size of dimes?" I asked.

He thought about it, then shook his head. "They'd be nice diamonds, but they sure as hell wouldn't be worth no ten million."

"Okay," I replied, unwilling to tell him anything more about the cat or the collar.

"That's it?"

"Not quite," I said. "There's one more thing."

"Yeah?"

"Yeah," I replied. "If they come in—dimes or golf balls—call me immediately."

"Eli, I love you like a long-lost brother," he said. "But I'm a businessman."

"Ziggy, you're a living businessman, and I want you to stay that way. These things are hotter than you can imagine."

"Who's after them?"

"Besides the owner?" I said. "I won't give you any names, but there are three shooters from South America and an enforcer from Chicago, just for starters."

His eyes widened. "You're not putting me on?"

I shook my head.

"Who else?" he asked.

"That's one of the things I'm trying to find out."

"Four shooters?"

"Three and one, right."

"If I get my hands on 'em, I'll just have to keep them on ice for a few years. They'll be my retirement gift to myself."

"Not a chance, Ziggy," I said. "These guys are all pros. They'll be here, the enforcer and the hitters, in the next day or two, as soon as they get the lay of the land or beat it out of some snitches. And if they don't find what they're looking for, ten million isn't the kind of thing that you shrug off and forget. They'll be back every couple of days, and one or the other will pay someone to keep an eye on you and the shop." I paused and stared at him. "You *don't* want to try and hide these stones from those men."

Ziggy was almost shaking when I got done.

"I'll take it under advisement," he said. "And thanks, Eli. You've always been a straight shooter with me. If I get them or hear of them, I'll be in touch so fast I'll feel like I'm back riding stakes horses at Keeneland again."

"Ziggy, I love you like a brother, too," I said. "But you never rode at Keeneland or anywhere else."

"Well, I *should* have," said the little fence. "But I could never make weight."

"It'll be our secret," I said, heading to the door.

"You going to the Goniff's?" he said. "We're rivals, but he's gotta know about this too."

I nodded. "He's next on my list."

Then I was out the door and walking back to my car. When I got there I found a parking ticket stuck under a wiper blade, tore it in half and deposited it in a nearby trash container like the good citizen I am, and headed a couple of miles west to Hegel the Goniff's jewelry shop, which was advertising a ten-thousand-dollar pearl necklace in the window and was as reasonable a front for a fence as you could want. I told him the same thing I'd told Ziggy, and since he'd been roughed up a couple of times by parties who didn't think possession was nine-tenths of the law, he agreed instantly to let me know if the diamonds showed up.

Finally I went back downtown and stopped by The Machine, a bar that was just down the street from Red's Jungle and was named back when the Reds *were* the Big Red Machine. I looked around, didn't see the man I was looking for, ordered a beer at the bar, and carried it over to a table. I'd nursed it for twenty minutes and most of a cigarette—my first of the day; well, first cigarette, not first beer—when the man I was waiting for walked in with a truly elegant redhead on his arm. He spotted me, parked the redhead at the bar, and walked over.

"Hi, Reuben," I said.

"Ruby, goddammit!"

"Hi, Ruby Goddammit," I amended. "You're moving up in the world. That's a gorgeous young lady you arrived with."

"Been trying to get her to come out for a drink for weeks. She finally agrees, and *you're* here. Make it quick."

"Three hitters arrived in town a couple of days ago. I need to know where they're staying, what names they're using, anything about them."

"Just three hitters, nothing else?" he said, frowning. "No connections to any of the families?"

"The only family they're connected to is in Bolivia."

He frowned again. "Bolivia?" he repeated.

"Right."

"They speak any English?"

"I don't know."

"How would I tell them from Mexicans?"

"I don't know," I said. "I haven't laid eyes on them."

"Then how the hell am I supposed—?"

"Just keep your ear to the ground," I said. "They'll probably travel together, they'll have money, and if they ask any questions, it'll be about a recent murder, a millionaire named Pepperidge."

"And that's everything you can give me?"

I nodded. "Just pass the word."

"There'll be the usual fee if I deliver?"

"Double," I said, figuring Sorrentino could cover it.

"Okay," he said. "Now, if you don't mind, I'd like to get back to my love life."

"Go," I said, finishing my beer.

"Aren't you going to wish me luck?"

I looked at the redhead again, then back at pudgy, out-of-shape Reuben. "You're going to need resuscitation more than luck."

He grinned. "Let's hope so."

Then he rejoined the redhead at the bar, I crossed his name off my mental list and went off to grab a four-way and a couple of cheese coneys at the nearest Skyline, thinking of Ziggy's Lincoln and Hegel's necklace and wondering why I'd become a detective instead of a fence.

8.

I phoned Val Sorrentino (and you wouldn't believe how difficult it is to find a pay phone in this day and age when everyone walks around with their own phones), and we agreed to meet at a nearby Steak 'n Shake. He was sitting at a booth when I got there, and the first thing I noticed was that he had a split lip and one eye was swollen shut.

"That's gonna be one hell of a shiner tomorrow," I said, sitting down and indicating his eye.

He shrugged. "It goes with the job."

"Maybe with *your* job," I said. "Who did it—one of the Bolivians?"

He smiled at that, then winced as his lip started bleeding. "They're shooters, not boxers."

"Then who?"

"I thought I spotted one of them, so I parked the car and started tailing him."

"He had protection?"

Sorrentino shook his head. "No. Some kid jumped out of an alley as I was crossing it, stuck a knife against my neck, and demanded my money."

"I don't see anything that looks like a knife did it," I noted.

He smiled again, then winced. "You're looking at the wrong guy." He paused long enough to wipe some blood from his lip. "I took the knife away from him and kind of carved my autograph on his jaw as a gentle reminder not to threaten strangers until you know something about them."

"Then what's with the eye and the lip?"

"He started screaming, and a couple of his friends jumped me before I could pull my gun." He shrugged. "Besides, I don't need the cops pinching me because of the gun and maybe asking their Chicago cousins about me."

"So what happened to his friends?" I asked.

"They should be waking up in another ten or twenty minutes," he said. "Unless someone calls an ambulance. Then they'll probably stay sedated until the doctors are through working on 'em."

"I'm glad you're on *my* side," I said devoutly.

"They were just a bunch of teenage assholes who thought they were tougher than they were," he replied. "I know a little about you—enough to know you can handle yourself better than they could."

I shrugged. Maybe I could ... but I didn't think I could handle myself well enough to make Val Sorrentino work up a sweat.

"So," he continued, "what have you learned?"

"Not much," I answered. "The diamonds haven't shown up at either of the two biggest local fences."

"Damn!" he muttered. "They haven't shown up with any of our associates either." He dabbed his lip again. "Anything else?"

"I had to warn my friend on the force about the Bolivians, but they have no record of them. Neither does the one snitch I've spoken to so far."

"Figures," said Sorrentino. "Cincinnati's not exactly a gateway city. People here would just figure they were legals or illegals from Mexico and never ask for a passport." He grimaced. "So we haven't made a lot of progress."

"We've warned our fences, the cops will call me if they spot the Bolivians, and I've got a snitch spreading the word." I paused and smiled. "And you've put three teenagers on the road to law-abiding adulthood."

"If they recover." He didn't smile, and I couldn't tell if he was kidding or not." He signaled a waitress. "Hey, babe—bring me a chocolate malt."

She nodded and went back to the tiny kitchen.

"Somehow I didn't picture you as a malt man," I said with a smile.

"I'd rather have a beer, but we're in a Steak 'n Shake," he admitted.

"Anyway, I can hold the glass against my eye and take down the swelling a bit, and then spread a little ice cream on my lip."

"You can just stop by an emergency room or an urgent care," I suggested.

He shook his head. "This is trivial. The emergency room is for the kid with the new tattoo on his face."

He seemed so friendly and open, it took the occasional remark like that one to remind me of just who I was dealing with.

"Well, there's one thing we know," I said. "Someone knew what the collar was worth, because they took it off the cat. My first thought was that it might have been a kid who just thought it was pretty, and if the cat had turned up at the nearest shelter I might still think so, but not when it shows up twenty miles away."

"You're the cop," said Sorrentino. "What do we do about it?"

"The ex-cop," I corrected him. "And what we do is make sure our fences know that they're likely to get killed if they put the diamonds on the market, or even tell anyone but you or me that they've got them."

"That makes sense if it was the Bolivians or some local hitter," he said, "but what if it was Velma? Maybe getting you arrested was just a cover?"

"That doesn't make sense. She doesn't know you're in town, so she can't have thought Palanto told you about the collar."

"If he told me, he could have told someone else. Velma hasn't got anything against killing a couple of dozen men if it suits her purposes, but she ain't as spry as she used to be, and she sure as hell isn't hard to describe or identify."

"If she killed him for the collar, then she'll kill anyone who's got it," I said. "Simple as that."

"What if she had some other reason for killing him?" suggested Sorrentino. "What if he was fooling around, or she was afraid of the Bolivian mob, or he wouldn't give her enough money to spend? Maybe the murder was the primary thing, and the collar was an afterthought."

"Makes no difference," I said. "Say she killed him because he smoked in bed or wouldn't turn the TV off at night. Say the collar was an afterthought. Based on everything you know about her, everything you've told me, would she stop at killing a fence, or half a dozen fences, to get her hands on the collar?"

He frowned. "No," he admitted. "No, she wouldn't."

"So it really boils down to who got their hands on the cat and took his collar off," I said.

He was about to reply when the waitress brought him his malt.

"Thanks, toots," he said, and this one didn't respond like the one in Bob Evans had to the name. "I'll take a glass of ice water too, more ice than water if you can manage it."

"You look like you need it," she said, staring at his eye. "I'll bring a rag you can wrap the ice in."

"How about you?" asked Sorrentino, turning to me. "My treat?"

"I'll take a double cheeseburger with onions and nothing else," I said. "And whatever kind of soda pop you have on hand, brand and flavor makes no difference."

"Like 'em all, eh?" she said with a smile and went back to the kitchen.

"So who took the collar off?" he said.

"I don't know," I answered. "Hell, I don't even know if the killer or the diamonds are still in town. It all depends."

"On what?"

"On who knew what the collar was worth besides you and Velma."

He frowned. "Are you accusing me?"

I shook my head. "No, I'm not. I'm just saying that if he told half a dozen people, then the collar could be in California or even Timbuktu by now. But if only you and Velma knew about it, then maybe the collar's still in town. Maybe someone's trying to find out what it's worth, who owns or owned it, what's likely to happen to him if he cashes in on it." I sighed. "Except . . ."

"Except what?"

"Except that it's too goddamned far-fetched," I said. "I just can't make myself think some passerby took one look, decided those were real twenty-carat or however many carat diamonds, picked up the cat, removed the collar, and then drove more than twenty miles through a blizzard just to dump the cat."

He sighed deeply. "It does sound kinda silly when you lay it out like that."

The waitress returned with his malt and ice. "Your burger'll be up in just a minute, hon," she told me. "Last chance to give me a hint: Coke or 7Up?"

I took a quick peek at the menu, ordered a High-C, and waited for her to move out of hearing range.

"That's why I think someone besides you and Velma knew. I just can't believe someone could spot and identify it in a blizzard . . . and I'll guarantee it was gone by four in the morning—and it wasn't just a blizzard; it was also a moonless night."

"You're making my head hurt," he said with a grimace. "That's something the Mike Tyson wannabe and his two buddies couldn't do."

"Stop making faces," I said. "Your lip's bleeding again."

He shrugged. "What's a little blood?"

"Not much, until it stains your shirt," I said. "How many did you bring to town?"

He looked down and saw the blood on his collar. "Shit!"

"What the hell," I said. "You're still standing. Maybe it'll scare people off."

"Fuck the blood," he said. "Let's get back to business."

"I thought we'd run through everything we know."

"I was following one of the Bolivians," he said. "When we're done here, I'm going back to where I spotted him and see if I can't pick up the trail again."

"Correction," I said. He stared curiously at me. "You *think* you were following one of the Bolivians."

He nodded. "Yeah, I think so."

"You know," I said after I thought about it for a few seconds, "I'm surprised they're not following *us*."

He looked puzzled. "What do you mean?"

"Think it through," I said. "If you're right about them, that they're here at all, they came to collect the money Palanto had siphoned off. Cordially if possible, but at any rate . . ."

He shook his head. "You don't send those guys on a cordial mission."

"I know," I said. "But bear with me for a minute. They came for the money. Let's say they killed him, and of course they didn't know about the cat. They're still in town, so clearly they're under orders not to go home without the money. They have no idea where it is, and by now someone in that organization knows it's not in a bank account. So it makes more sense for them to be following the Chicago contact and the Cincinnati detective than for us to be following them. If you just stand still, they'll show up."

"Eli, you don't *want* those bastards showing up on their own terms," said Sorrentino. "Trust me on that. From what our friends in Mexico told us, they've made more than twenty kills outside their own country."

"They may rough us up, but they're not going to kill us as long as they think we might know where the diamonds are."

He shook his head. "They don't know from shit about diamonds. And if you prefer being tortured for a few days rather than killed, my hat's off to you, but that ain't *my* notion of a good way to go." Suddenly he frowned again. "We're overlooking something."

"Oh?" I said.

"Yeah. Their people have the clout to know there's nothing worthwhile in Palanto's bank account, and that he hasn't got a ton on deposit anywhere else. But why not stash it in a safe deposit box?"

"You say there are three shooters, but so far you've only seen one," I pointed out. "It makes sense that at least one of them is watching Velma around the clock . . . and if she's made no move to go to a bank or any place else with a lock box, and she's not leaving town, they probably figure she hasn't got it, and they'll be more sure of that every day that she sticks around."

"Shit!" he muttered. "I guess that's why you're the detective." He downed about half his malt, then pressed the glass against his eye as the waitress brought my burger and drink. "So what's our next move?"

"There's not much we *can* do until the diamonds show up or someone makes a very discernible move to get their hands on 'em," I answered. "I suppose I'll contact all the minor-league fences, talk to some more snitches, and we'll try to find the Bolivians, who are probably watching us while we're watching out for the diamonds."

"And that's all?" he asked. "I mean, I know you've solved a couple of pretty complex cases . . ."

"One of them took me over a month and got me beat up hundreds of miles south of the Mexican border," I pointed out. "The other wasn't exactly a piece of cake either. We're not talking a crime of passion here, Val. At least, not necessarily. All we know is that someone killed Big Jim Palanto, and the diamonds are missing. But we don't know *who* killed him or *why*, and because of that, we don't know if the diamonds were the motive or had anything to do with it."

He looked dubious. "Of course they did," he said as I bit into my sandwich.

I shook my head. "Not necessarily. For all you know, the Bolivians are here as a punishment party." He started to protest, but I held up a hand. "Yeah, I know, they're still here, hoping somehow that you or someone will lead them to the money. But since they didn't know about the cat, and there were no marks on the corpse, it's clear they didn't try beating the information out of him, and it's just as clear he wasn't running away from them, not on his balcony in a blizzard."

"Shit!" he said. "I hate it when you make sense."

"Same thing with Velma," I continued. "She knew about the collar. So if that's what she was after, she didn't have to kill him to get her hands on it. The cat lived in the same house. All she had to do was wait 'til Palanto was out or sleeping and just remove it. So if she killed him, it also wasn't for the money."

"But she had you thrown in the can!" he protested.

"Wouldn't you, if you thought I'd stolen ten million bucks from you?"

"Shit!" he said again, loud enough to attract some attention from neighboring tables.

"Yeah, I know," I said with a smile. "You hate it when I make sense."

"But it *had* to be one or the other!" he growled. "She could have had half a dozen reasons to want him dead, and she knew what the collar was worth. And they came to collect their money and punish him for stealing it. Who the hell else is there?"

"If I give you a couple of possibilities, will you admit this isn't an open-and-shut case with only two suspects?"

"Four," he said. "There are three Bolivians."

"You know what I mean," I said.

He stared at me, frowning. "Okay, let's hear it. Who else could it have been?"

"The man who sold him the diamonds," I said. "The man who mounted them onto the collar. The vet who recognized that they weren't rhinestones."

"Not the vet," said Sorrentino. "He couldn't know he was dealing with Big Jim Palanto."

"He didn't have to," I pointed out. "Malcolm Pepperidge is living in a house that has to be worth over a million."

He sighed deeply. "I am starting to dislike you intensely," he said, only half-joking. "Do you have a fucking answer to *every*thing?"

"Hey," I said. "*I* don't live in a million-dollar palace. My rent is five hundred a month, and I'm late on it. And I'm driving a twelve-year-old Ford that needs a transmission job. I'm wrong more often than I care to think about."

"I'm sorry," he said. "Really. It's just so frustrating. Back home the boss says, 'Lean on this guy' and I go lean on him. I don't have to ask if it's the right guy, or how hard to lean, or what's he done to deserve what I'm gonna do to him, or anything like that. I just lean on the son of a bitch." He paused and shook his head. "I wouldn't trade jobs with you for anything."

I finished my burger while he was talking. "Well, every profession has its hazards," I said. "Maybe I don't make much money, but hardly anyone ever wants to arrest me for doing my job right."

Suddenly he laughed. "Unless her name is Velma."

I nodded my head. "Unless her name is Velma," I agreed.

"You know," he said thoughtfully, "maybe I should lean on her. She's never seen me. She might guess who I work for, but she doesn't know. Maybe I can make sure one way or the other."

"Make sure of what?" I asked.

He frowned. "If she killed him."

"Okay," I said. "Say she did. So what?"

He just stared at me uncomprehendingly.

"Val," I continued, "we're not trying to solve the damned murder. We're looking for the diamonds, and we already know she doesn't have them and doesn't know where they are."

"Shit!"

"Someday I'm going to have to teach you a new word," I said.

He gave me an embarrassed grin. "I'm sorry."

"Not a problem." I checked my watch. "Okay, we'd better get back to work. I'll check with some more fences, you see if you can find out what names the Bolivians are using and where they're staying."

"Doesn't seem like much," he said. "Is there anything else I can do?"

"Maybe," I said. "*Someone* had to sell him ten million dollars' worth of diamonds, and given the size of a cat's collar, I figure that's ten diamonds, tops. There can't have been many diamonds that size up for sale, legit sale or under the counter, at one time. See if any of your people know about a sale that size."

"Right," he said. "Should be easy enough."

"You think so?"

"Sure," replied Sorrentino. "Why not?"

"What if he bought the diamonds seven years ago? Or on a European vacation? Or—?"

"Okay!" he half-shouted. "I get the picture!"

"Anyway," I continued, "it's probably a dead end, but it's worth looking into."

"I know," he said. "Sorry I shouted. I just wasn't cut out to be a detective."

"There's those who say the same about me," I said.

He picked up the check where the waitress had dropped it, walked over to the cash register, handed the guy a twenty, and told him to keep the change. Then we both walked outside.

"I'm parked that way," he said, pointing to the left. "You?"

I gestured to the right.

"Call me later and we'll meet for dinner," he said, heading off.

I stood watching him for a minute, half expecting to see one or more Bolivians leap out from between buildings and take a few shots at him, but nothing happened, and finally I turned and went to my car, wondering for the hundredth time if the cat had been turned in to the shelter by an animal lover or a diamond lover.

9.

I drove home, woke Marlowe long enough to take him for a walk, which he resented like all hell, then drove downtown to my office to see if I'd accumulated any mail in the past few days. Twenty-seven ads, an electric bill, and a letter from a Mrs. Karbasso, who didn't care that the Communist threat was over everywhere else and *knew* there was a Communist living inside her walls watching her every move. She apologized for not having any money but offered to pay me with a lemon pie once I sent this foul fiend off to meet his ancestors.

I put my feet up on the desk, clasped my hands behind my head, leaned back, and considered what to do next. I found it difficult to think of it as a case, since no one was paying me, but since I didn't have any other cases pending and I still had most of Velma's fifteen-hundred-dollar retainer, I decided I could give it a couple of more days.

The problem was: a couple of days doing *what*?

I couldn't look for the diamonds, because first of all, I didn't know what they looked like; second, I didn't know if they were on or off the collar; and third, they were in a metropolitan area of well over a million.

I couldn't question the Bolivians. No one knew where they were or what names they were using. Besides, from what Sorrentino had told me, they were every bit as likely to shoot me as talk to me.

I couldn't question Velma. The second she saw me she'd call the cops and have me arrested for trespassing or harassment.

I could talk to Ziggy and the Goniff again, but I'd just spoken to them that morning. Same with Reuben.

I could make the rounds of the top jewelers, but I'd feel silly as hell asking them if they'd attached ten million dollars' worth of diamonds to a cat collar.

So what, I wondered, could I do that wasn't 100 percent useless or idiotic?

I thought about it for a few minutes and came up with a notion that was perhaps only 98 percent idiotic.

I swiveled the chair until it was facing my typewriter, stuck a sheet of paper in it, and began typing:

Will the party that found my mackerel tabby cat and turned it in to the Wilkinson Animal Shelter two days ago please contact me? I want to thank you in person and present you with a gift for finding her.

I closed by putting in my home phone number—just in case someone was being exceptionally careful, I didn't want them to figure out they were calling a detective. Then I stared at it for a couple of minutes and decided it lacked a little something.

Finally I folded the paper, stuck it in my lapel pocket, closed up the office, and drove home, which took all of fifteen minutes, and found that the mail wasn't any more interesting there than at the office.

"Why aren't you out tracking criminals?" said a familiar voice, and I turned to find myself facing Mrs. Cominsky.

I was about to give her a sarcastic answer when I suddenly realized that she might be just what I needed.

"How would you like to help me on a case, Mrs. Cominsky?" I said.

"Are you after a killer or a rapist?" she asked enthusiastically.

"I don't know," I said.

She frowned. "What do you mean?"

"I'm after either a killer or a good Samaritan."

"Are you making fun of me?" she demanded suspiciously.

I shook my head. "Not at all. If I can prove it's a killer, then I'll turn it over to the cops. But I've got to talk to him or her first."

"Well, come on in," she said, suddenly businesslike. "No sense doing this in a freezing foyer." I walked through the inner door to the staircase. "My place or yours?"

"Mine, I think," I said. "We have your reputation to consider."

I led the way up to the second-floor landing, unlocked my door, and stood aside while she entered first. Marlowe looked up, said, *Oh, it's you*, yawned, and went back to sleep.

"All right, Mr. Paxton," she said. "How can I help you?"

"Someone turned a cat in to an animal shelter the other day," I said. "And it's essential that I find him."

She frowned. "That damned cat again?" she said. "Someone's really paying you to find it?" She shook her head, half in disbelief, half in contempt for my employer.

"It's *been* found," I said.

"So what is all this about?" she demanded.

"I need to find who turned it in to the shelter."

"Ah! The thief!"

"Maybe," I said. "If it's the person who stole it, we could be looking at a murderer. But if it's just some guy who found it and brought it to the shelter, then like I said, it's a Samaritan."

"Why some *guy*?" she asked in a way that implied that I was a male chauvinist pig, which I probably am from time to time. "Why not a woman?"

"Because the lady at the shelter told me it was a guy," I answered.

"Okay, some guy gave the cat to the shelter, and maybe he's a killer, and maybe he's just a good Christian," said Mrs. Cominsky. "What does that have to do with me?"

"I wrote an ad as if I was the owner, hoping he'd make contact with me. But I think it could be a little better, or at least a little more *sincere*. I was hoping that if I show it to you that you might make a suggestion or two."

"Ah!" she said happily, now that we were getting down to business. "Let me see it!"

I pulled the paper out, unfolded it, and handed it to her. She studied it for a moment, a frown of either concentration or disapproval written large across her face.

"Well?" I asked when she looked up.

"First of all, the cat needs a name."

"Fluffy," I told her.

She took a pencil out of a pocket and scribbled the name down on the paper.

"And she's not your mackerel tabby," she said. "She's your *beloved* mackerel tabby."

"Okay," I said, as she wrote it down. "Anything else?"

"Yes," she said. "He turned *her* in, not *it*. Beloved cats are never its." She scribbled again. "Also, he didn't *find* her; he saved her. And maybe a heart-felt gift, rather than just a gift. You don't want to say a valuable gift or you'll get three hundred jerks calling and pretending they turned the cat in."

She finished writing and handed it back to me:

Will the party who found my beloved mackerel tabby cat Fluffy and turned her in to the Wilkinson Animal Shelter two days ago please contact me? I want to thank you in person and present you with a heart-felt gift for saving her.

"Well?" she asked.

"Better," I said. "Let's hope it works."

"Now that we're partners," she said, "who was killed and what does the cat have to do with it?"

"The police have asked me not to divulge the name of the deceased to anyone," I lied. "And the cat may have nothing at all to do with it."

She frowned again. "Why would a killer take a victim's cat with him? It's not as if the damned thing could testify to what it saw."

I shrugged. "I don't know. Maybe it scratched him, maybe he got some DNA on it."

She shook her head. "Then why turn it in to a shelter?"

"If I had all the answers I'd know who he was and he'd be in jail or totally off the hook," I said.

"Let's put our heads together and see what we can reason out."

"Not this second," I said apologetically. "I can tell Marlowe needs a walk. Can't have him messing the rug," I said as I grabbed his leash and put it on him.

"The carpet, damn it!" she snapped.

"Back soon," I said as I opened the door and tugged Marlowe, who was still nine-tenths asleep, down the stairs and out the door.

It was still light out, and I walked Marlowe almost two blocks past Mrs. Garabaldi's petunias in the hope that Mrs. Cominsky would get tired of waiting for me, but she'd had an evangelistic look about her face as I left that said, *You're Nick, I'm Nora, that's Asta, and we're going to solve a murder that's stumped the police.*

Even Marlowe, who never feels anything, was getting uncomfortably cold, and finally I began walking him back to the apartment. I became aware that a car was following us very slowly the final half block. I figured it was just because of some icy patches on the street, but then I remembered I'd just driven on the same street maybe half an hour ago, and the traction was fine, so I stopped and turned to look at it.

It was a BMW, and the driver had coal-black hair, dark eyes, a black mustache, and a deep tan, either natural or from the sun.

Suddenly he smiled, pointed his finger at me, and fired an imaginary shot between my eyes.

"Marlowe," I said as he raced off, "I think I've just seen my first Bolivian."

10.

"Now *this* is a *real* dinner!" enthused Sorrentino as we were eating at Carrabba's. "Reminds me of the old country!"

"Come on, Val," I said. "When were you in the old country?"

"Three, four years ago," he said. "And to tell you the truth, their shrimp scampi doesn't compare to this." He shrugged. "Hell, I don't know why all Italians talk about the old country. If it was so damned good, we wouldn't have come here, would we?"

"I don't know where the hell the Paxtons came from," I said. "If they didn't change the name at Ellis Island, I suspect we were British peasants."

"How many generations ago?"

"Beats the hell out of me," I replied.

"You never asked?" he said, surprised.

I shook my head. "It never interested me. Wherever we came from a century or two ago, I'm not going back."

"A man's gotta know where he came from," said Sorrentino.

"I'm more concerned with where I'm going." I took a swallow of my beer. "And who's trying to stop me."

He stared at me and frowned. "What are you talking about?"

"I'm pretty sure I saw one of the Bolivians a couple of hours ago, when I was walking my dog."

"What was he doing?"

"Just driving his car, at maybe five miles an hour, pacing me as I walked."

"Could have been anyone," said Sorrentino.

"Could have," I said.

"But you don't think so?"

"No."

"Okay, why?"

I aimed my finger at him and fired an imaginary shot.

"He did that?" asked Sorrentino.

"Right," I said.

He frowned. "Doesn't make sense."

"It made perfect sense to me," I said. "He's warning me off the case."

He shook his head vigorously. "If he knows where you live, he knows you're private, and that means you're not after the killer, you're after the money. Why the hell would he warn you off? He ought to be explaining to you that he'll ride shotgun while you hunt for it and let you keep one-third of it. Of course, if you agreed and found it, he'd kill you, but why threaten you *before* you find it?"

"I think he was just letting me know he's here, and that he and his friends are going to be mighty pissed off if I find the money and don't offer to share with them, maybe ninety-ten in their favor."

"Maybe," he said, unconvinced. "But if he's keeping an eye on you, why didn't he follow you to the restaurant?"

"There are three of them. Maybe one of the others did. All I was looking for in my rearview was his BMW."

"Makes sense," he said.

I finished my veal parmesan, washed it down with the rest of the beer, considered having my first smoke of the day, couldn't see an ashtray anywhere in the place, suddenly remembered that you can't smoke in restaurants in Cincinnati, and settled for watching Sorrentino finish his shrimp.

"So what's our next move, Mr. Detective?" he said when he was done eating.

"I've been thinking about it," I said. I checked my watch. "Quarter after seven. I think I can start in a few minutes."

"Doing what?"

"I'm going to take my dog for a walk."

He stared at me. "Enough with the jokes."

"I'm not joking."

"Then what the hell *are* you doing, Eli?" he demanded.

"Laying the groundwork," I said.

Suddenly his face lit up. "This has something to do with the Bolivian who spotted you!"

"Right," I said.

"You want him to see you again, and that's why you're walking the dog. OK, I got that much. But then what? You're sure as hell not looking to get into a shootout with him. Hell, he might have both his stablemates with him."

"I leave the shootouts to John Wayne and Clint Eastwood," I said. "Once I know he's following me, I'm going to walk to my car, toss Marlowe in it—"

"Marlowe?" he interrupted me.

"My dog. Then I'm going to drive downtown."

"And then what?"

"And then I'm going to report him to the cops, who are looking for him anyway."

"He'll just drive off."

I smiled at him. "I don't think so."

"You know something I don't know," he said.

"Hell, if push comes to shove, I probably know three or four things you don't know."

"Just the same, I'd better ride shotgun."

"I told you: I don't want a shootout," I said. "Val, I know what I'm doing. If he didn't shoot me when he saw me walking Marlowe before, he's not going to shoot me now. He's just keeping an eye on me, and maybe trying to make sure I know he's willing to shoot me under the right circumstances . . . but those circumstances aren't tonight."

"You're sure?" he asked.

"I'm sure."

"So what do *I* do while you're pulling off whatever the hell it is you're pulling off?"

"Meet me at police headquarters." I told him how to get there, then checked my watch again and did the math. "Meet me there in an hour."

"At the police station?" he said, frowning.

I nodded. "Just walk in the door. I'll be waiting for you."

The waiter came by with the check, and Sorrentino grabbed it before I could (not that I tried very hard).

"I make a lot more money busting heads than you do saving 'em," he said. "I'm paying for any meals we eat together until we find the money or give up looking for it."

I decided to not even pretend to protest.

"I hope you know what you're doing, Eli," he said as the waiter made change. "Keep it, son," he said, waving the fortyish waiter off. "How long do I wait if you're not there?"

"If I'm not there by eleven, go to bed and get some sleep, because it means our Bolivian friend wasn't as interested in me as we think."

We got up and walked to the door.

"Take care of yourself," he said, walking off to his car.

I went over to the Ford, started it up, and headed the four miles home. Marlowe wasn't thrilled to see me, and he was even less thrilled to be dragged out into the cold, especially since we were being visited with a freezing drizzle.

I walked him to his favorite urinal—Mrs. Garabaldi's petunias—but she must have been busy watching television, because for a change there was no cursing. I looked around, hoping to see a car tracking me, but there was no traffic on the street.

"Show up, damn it!" I muttered. "I'm freezing my ass off."

So was Marlowe, who tried to pull me back to the apartment. He turned to growl his displeasure at me, got tangled in the leash, and as I squatted down to unwrap him I spotted it, parked about twenty yards away. Same BMW as before, and I could see now that it had a man—doubtless my Bolivian, or one of his partners, seated behind the wheel, just keeping a watchful eye on me.

Marlowe saw the front door to the apartment and began tugging for all he was worth.

"Hey, pal," I said, pulling him toward the car. "Wanna go for a ride?"

He gave me a look that said, *Are you crazy?* and pulled back as hard as he could. Finally I just leaned over, picked him up, and tossed him onto the backseat, then walked around to the driver's side, opened the door, and got in. I could see that the BMW had started its motor—I couldn't hear it, and the lights weren't on yet, but I could see vapor coming out of its tailpipe. I started the car, gave it a moment to warm up, mostly so the BMW, which was facing the wrong direction, had time to turn around in an alley.

I checked my watch. Just a few minutes from eight o'clock. Yeah, I'd be right on schedule. I turned left, the BMW followed me, I turned right a few blocks later, he did the same, and I gradually made my way downtown. When I was within a mile I turned on the radio to hear the latest sports news and to confirm that I'd made the right decision. There was a bit about an upcoming middleweight title fight, some shortstop was going public about being disrespected since he'd only been offered seventy million to sign for three years, and then came what I was waiting for: there was a huge rally for the Bengals at Paul Brown Stadium starting at eight-thirty, and traffic was stop and go, the rain was coming down a little harder, visibility could have been better, and even as I was listening and approaching the stadium I got caught in the stop-and-go traffic I was hearing about.

I stopped, fourth in line, at a red light at the corner of 6th and Vine. My passenger's door opened and Jim Simmons climbed in.

"Glad you got my message," I said.

"I wish to hell you'd learn to use a cell phone," he said bitterly. "I've been standing out here in this shit for half an hour waiting for you to show up. There must be ten thousand cars here. It's almost as bad as game day, and that wind!" He shuddered, then damned near jumped through the roof when Marlowe barked at him.

"What the hell is *that*?" he demanded.

"Marlowe."

"Seriously, Eli."

"Seriously. He's my dog. That's his name."

"And you brought him along for protection?" he said sardonically.

"I brought him along because I was afraid if I went into the apartment to put him away they'd think I wasn't coming back out and maybe go home for the night."

"Then he *is* following you?"

"The blue BMW right behind me," I said.

"Okay, we're in business." Simmons pulled out his cell phone. "Hello, Bill? It's working. We're at 6th and Vine. Fifth car at the light is a BMW, almost certainly rented, and the license plate is"—he read off the number. "Send a couple of traffic cops over to give him a ticket, have him get out of the car while they act as if they're about to inspect it, and the second he's out, cuff him." He paused. "The car? All right, get a third man to drive it to the station. This guy may be a killer. Even with cuffs on him, I want at least two cops with him. Right."

He put the cell phone away. "Okay, Eli," he said. "Unless you've got an overwhelming urge to listen to the players taking turns predicting that they'll beat the Steelers on Sunday, turn north and let's get over to the station."

We arrived about ten minutes later. The traffic had thinned as we got a mile north of the Ohio River, which ran by both stadiums. I parked in the police lot, and Jim and I entered just as they were leading the Bolivian to a holding cell.

He turned and saw me enter. I flashed him a smile, then pointed my finger at him and fired it.

If looks could kill, I'd have been dead two seconds later.

11.

Sorrentino had been waiting for me at the station, as we'd arranged, and Simmons told us both to go home and that he'd call me in the morning after the cops had learned what they could. Since it was a choice between that and sitting in the station's lobby all night, I took his advice and headed back to my car.

"Cops make me nervous," complained Sorrentino, who was walking alongside me. "I take my hat off to you, Eli. You said they'd pull him in, and sonuvabitch, they did."

I smiled. "They don't play football in Bolivia."

"They play soccer, but they call it football," he sort-of agreed.

"They don't have rallies that turn out half the city before they play the Steelers or the Ravens," I said. "I knew if he followed me we'd be in a stop-and-go jam—well, a stop-and-almost-stop—and then, since Simmons knew I was on my way and the Bolivian was following me, it was nothing to call a couple of cops while we were all standing still."

"Damn!" he exclaimed, and then grinned. "Maybe there's something to not shooting first."

"If you're as bad a shot as I am, there's a lot to recommend it," I answered.

He laughed at that. "You got a point."

We reached my car. "Can I drop you somewhere?" I asked him.

"No," he replied. "I'm parked about half a block up ahead." He looked in a window and frowned. "You got something in the backseat?"

I knocked on the window, and Marlowe was up and barking furiously half a second later.

"Yeah, *that'll* make any car thief think twice."

"Unless they growl back at him," I said. "Then he'll hide under the mat."

He looked at Marlowe and made a face. Marlowe looked right back at him and made a face; Marlowe's had more teeth in it.

"Okay," he said. "We might as well be going. You'll contact me after you hear from your friend?"

"Yeah," I said. "I'll go home, walk the dog once more, and go to bed so I won't sleep through Simmons's call in the morning."

"I'll stop by a bar for a drink or two and think about you freezing your ass off walking Mike Hammer."

"Marlowe," I corrected him.

He shrugged. "Whatever."

Then he was heading toward his car. I walked around to the driver's door, unlocked it, told Marlowe to get his front feet off the window, stop growling, and lie down, and began driving home.

I half-expected to find that one of the other Bolivians was tailing me, but there was no one within a block of me all the way home. Someone had taken my parking place, and I had to park almost a block from my front door, but it just meant that Marlowe got a little longer walk than usual.

When we got to the apartment I took his leash off, he raced to the couch, leaped on it, and dared me to move him. I went to the kitchen to see what I had in the fridge for a little snack before I went to bed. There was a half-gallon of three-week-old milk, half a pizza that had been sitting there for a week, and a couple of other things.

I didn't see anything that appealed to me—par for the course in my refrigerator—when I became aware of the fact that I was not alone.

Cold pizza? said Marlowe. *What a good idea!*

"Okay," I said. "But if I share the pizza with you, you got to share the couch with me."

He wasn't thrilled with the arrangement, but finally he agreed and we sat down together with the pizza between us. I picked up the remote to see what was on TCM. It was *The Mask of Dimitrios* with Peter Lorre and Sydney Greenstreet, just the kind of charming and unarmed criminals I never seemed to run into in the real world. We finished the pizza just about the time Sydney shot Zachary Scott, and a couple of minutes later the end credits rolled, and shortly after that it was Robert Mitchum and Jane Greer in *The Big Steal*. I think I figured out the plot about ten minutes into it, but I fell asleep before I could be sure, and I slept through the next few movies until the phone woke me up.

I got to my feet, which really pissed Marlowe off since he'd been snoring on my lap, turned off the TV, and walked to the phone.

"Yeah?" I croaked.

"Eli? It's Jim."

"What did you learn?" I asked.

"You're not gonna believe this, but he was traveling on a passport that says his name is Sam Smith. The other two are Joe Smith and Jim Smith, and they're college professors." He laughed. "What do you think of that?"

"I think they're killers," I replied. "Just incredibly stupid ones, or at least uncreative ones. What did you find out about them?"

"Not much. They're staying at a Motel 6 out in the suburbs, but when he didn't show up last night I'm sure they figured out we had him and moved to a new place."

"Can you hold him for a while?"

"Not a problem," he said. "Our friend Señor Smith was carrying not one, not two, but three guns, plus what we used to call a switchblade. There's no Bolivian consulate here, so I asked if he wanted us to inform the one in Chicago." He laughed. "He shook his head so hard I thought his mustache might fly off. But the interesting thing is he didn't correct me."

I frowned. "Correct you?"

"Eli, he's traveling on a Paraguayan passport. I'll lay plenty of five-to-one that he's never set foot in Paraguay in his life."

"I wouldn't bet the farm on that, Jim," I said. "He and his almost-brothers are probably sent all over South America to kill anyone their family's not happy with."

"You're right, of course," said Simmons. "I'll wire his prints to Bolivia and Paraguay and see who's got anything on him. I'm getting a little long in the tooth. I was going to say that you shoot the wrong guy in Uruguay or Paraguay and you find yourself in a war with a couple of hundred former Nazis . . . but I guess they're all dead of old age by now, aren't they?"

"Let's hope so," I said. "Anything else about Mr. Smith?"

"Nope."

"May I make a suggestion?"

"Sure," said Simmons.

"Mention Big Jim Palanto to him and see what he does."

"You got it," he said. "I've been up all night. As soon as I get some sleep, I'll go back and try it out."

"Okay," I said. "I'll be in touch."

I sat back down on the couch. The TV was showing *The Three Stooges*, who never appealed to me, so I left the sound off and thought I'd grab another couple hours of sleep, when Marlowe decided to strengthen his teeth by chewing on my shoe, which happened to be on my foot, so after a couple of minutes I growled back at him, put on my coat, attached his leash to his collar, and took him out for a walk.

I wasn't fifty feet from the front door when I realized I was being watched by another Bolivian Smith. He was sitting in a tan Audi, pretending to read a newspaper, but I could see him peeking at me over the top of it.

"Okay," I muttered. "Let's see how serious you are."

I walked to the corner, turned right, walked another two blocks, then entered an old apartment building, and sat on the floor by the mailbox. Marlowe was sure I was inventing a new game, but after failing to get me to show him the rules he finally sighed and laid down. I sat there for an hour, then got up and walked back to my apartment—and sure enough he was gone. Probably driving all the hell over the neighborhood looking for me.

It meant two things. One, they wanted to know who I was seeing. And two, they may have been good at killing, but thinking wasn't their long and strong suit.

Since I was up and awake, I figured I might as well check in with Sorrentino, so I phoned him and made arrangements to meet for lunch at a different Bob Evans since I couldn't be sure "Toots" wouldn't dump a bowl of soup on his head if he called her that again.

"Joe Smith, Jim Smith, and Sam Smith," he repeated in wonderment, shaking his head. "We ain't playing with any mental giants here. Did your pal Simmons get anything else out of whichever the hell Smith he's got locked up?"

"Not as of eight-thirty this morning," I said.

"That was three hours ago," he said pulling his cell phone out and handing it to me. "Try him again."

"He was up all night," I replied. "He's home sleeping."

"You've been working in this town for half a dozen years," he said. "Surely you got more than one friend on the force."

"True," I responded. "But I only have one who was questioning our Bolivian friend."

"Well, at least find out how the hell long they can keep him," he urged.

"Okay," I said, staring at the phone. "I'll call the department. Show me how the damned thing works."

"Just give me a number," he said. "I'll call it and hand it over to you when it starts ringing."

I gave him the number of Jim's department, and a few seconds later he nodded and gave me the phone.

"Hello," I said. "This is Eli Paxton."

"Hi, Eli," said the voice at the other end. "This is Bill Calhoun."

"Hi, Bill," I said. "You still got our Bolivian visitor?"

"Mr. Smith?" he said with a chuckle. "Yeah, he's still here. I think we're waiting for orders to deport him, though of course we'll keep all his artillery."

"He's got two companions who are just as dangerous and are still on the loose. Can you hold him another day or two?"

He sighed audibly. "Jim said the same thing. What the hell, he's not lawyered up and he's probably here illegally. We can probably hold him another week if we have to."

"I really appreciate it."

"Happy to," he replied. "But that's the limit until we can file a charge. We've sent off a message to the Bolivian authorities to see if the guns are registered there. Now, and since they were concealed in his closed car and he never pulled them on the guys who arrested him, he'll probably walk on a conceal-carry charge. But I'm sure we can hold him on using a phony passport, plus whatever he's wanted for in South America. I gather we're returning him as soon as we find out what he's got to do with the local Mexican drug gangs."

"Not a damned thing in this instance," I said. "Anyway, I just need a little more time to hunt down his friends."

"We're working on that too," said Calhoun. "But we're being, I dunno, *subtle* about it, since they also haven't broken any laws."

Except maybe murder, I wanted to say, but stopped myself in time. I appear like a fool to enough people without going out of my way to add more.

I thanked him again, gave the phone back to Sorrentino since I didn't know how to hang it up, and answered his questions, which concerned the half of the conversation he hadn't heard.

"So," I concluded, "we've got twenty-four hours to find them before the one in jail is turned loose and they probably all change names and passports."

"I don't know . . ." he began.

"Okay," I said, "I give up. What don't you know?"

"I don't know if I want to find them."

"Oh?"

"We know they don't have the money, or they'd be gone. So we're looking for it, and they're looking for it, and our interests are the same. Now, I have no personal reason not to kill them if push comes to shove, but I don't want to start a war between Chicago and Sucre."

"Sucre?" I repeated.

"The capitol of Bolivia." He finished his coffee. "I think I'm going to leave it to you to track them down, if you can. If I'm with you and things start getting hairy, I just don't want to be responsible."

"But it's okay if they shoot me?" I said.

"So don't go looking for them," said Sorrentino. "We know they don't have the money. Hell, the way they're following you, they either think you have it or that you'll lead them to it."

"Do you think they killed Palanto?" I asked him.

He shrugged. "Who cares? The *money* is the important thing."

I could see his point of view, but I had different priorities. I figured the important thing was to make sure they weren't going to shoot me if they thought I was getting close to the money, because if I was out of the way they could just follow whatever trail I was on, and it would lead them to the pot of gold (well, of diamonds).

He paid for lunch, and I agreed to meet him for dinner at a new Greek place on the northeast side. Then he went to his car, I went to mine, and I tried to justify in my mind that the main reason I wanted to find the two remaining Bolivians before their companion was released from jail and maybe carrying a serious grudge against me, wasn't to solve a murder but to arrange a truce so I could hunt for the diamonds without looking over my shoulder every two steps.

12.

I checked in with my fences and my snitch, added three more snitches to the list, and finally couldn't think of another thing to do before dinner, so I went home to take a nap. Marlowe quickly explained to me that napping was *his* job and feeding the dog was *mine*. I opened a can of SpaghettiOs for him, decided to sprawl out on the couch while he was eating, and fell asleep to the dulcet tones of Chris Berman's maniacal screaming as he dramatized every play, especially the dull ones, from last weekend's football games on ESPN. I'd just dozed off when Marlowe finished the SpaghettiOs, wandered into the living room, hopped up onto the couch (which meant onto my stomach), decided it wasn't comfortable enough, and began trying to dig out a little hole to lie down in. I waved a groggy hand in his direction, hoping I could knock him off me without waking up any further, and all I got for my trouble was a dog clinging to my shirtsleeve as it hung above the floor.

"All right, goddammit!" I muttered, sitting up and making room for him. He decided he wanted the side I was sitting on, and we changed places. He was probably snoring thirty seconds before I was.

I woke up an hour and a half later, checked my watch, and decided that it was just about time to drive up to the Greek joint. I considered walking Marlowe first, but as I approached him I elicited a growl that said *I am sound asleep and woe betide the fool who wakes me*, so I hung the leash on a doorknob, put on my coat, and walked out to the car.

There wasn't much traffic, and I got there about twenty minutes early. I'd just finished a beer and was starting on a Greek coffee, which tasted exactly like American coffee only, well, Greek, when Sorrentino showed up.

"Any news?" he asked.

I shook my head. "How about you?"

"Not a thing."

"How long is your family going to let you stay here?" I asked. "After all, Palanto can't testify against them."

"Another few days," he said. Suddenly he grinned. "I told them I was recruiting you."

"That'll be great for business when it gets out," I said.

"You haven't got all that much business that I can see," he replied. "I guess it's feast or famine when you're private heat."

"Not always," I replied. "There's a guy in town named Bill Striker. Got the biggest detective agency in the city, maybe in the state. For some it's feast and more feast."

"Maybe we should let him in on this deal," suggested Sorrentino.

"Val, we don't *have* a deal," I said. "And you don't want to invite a millionaire detective who protects rock stars and athletes and other expensive things to help us find some diamonds that aren't ours."

"You see?" he said with a smile. "I keep saying you're the bright one."

We really didn't have any other information to exchange, so we spent the rest of the meal talking about the Bears and the Bengals—I suppose if it had been summer it would have been the Cubs and the Reds—and finally we pigged out on baklava and made arrangements to meet for lunch at a Texas Roadhouse, just to be different.

I drove back to the apartment, forcibly woke Marlowe, and even more forcibly took him for a walk, couldn't spot either of the remaining Bolivians, and got back inside just before it started snowing.

"Snow, rain, snow," I muttered to the god of weather. "I wish to hell you'd make up your mind."

I raced Marlowe for the couch, lost, went into the kitchen to make some coffee, realized I hadn't shaved in three days, and stopped by the bathroom to apply some shaving cream. I tried not to cut myself too many times and finally sat down on the portion of the couch he'd left for me.

I was never a Barbara Stanwyck fan, but TCM was running *The*

G-String Murders, in which Barbara, as Gypsy Rose Lee, shows how even a stripper can solve a murder that baffles the cops and the private eyes. When Pinky Lee came on doing some burlesque clown routine, I gave in to an irresistible urge to watch a documentary on gecko lizards, which were better-looking and seemed somewhat brighter than the average baggy-pants comic.

I was just about to doze off again when the phone rang.

"Yeah?" I said.

"This is Ruby," said the familiar voice of my head snitch.

"You got something for me?"

"Maybe so, maybe not."

"Give me the maybe so first," I said.

"Two guys named Smith checked into the Cincinnatian this afternoon."

"Joe and Jim?"

"I'm working on that."

"OK, what's the maybe not part?"

I could almost see him shrug. "Maybe they're two gay guys out to have a good anonymous time."

"In Cincinnati's answer to the Waldorf or the Palmer House?" I said.

"Maybe they're paying for discretion."

"I don't suppose you got a room number?"

"There's just so much you can get out of a place like that."

"Okay," I said. "And thanks."

"If it's them, I did this for more than verbal thanks."

"If it's them, I'll find a proper way to thank you, Reuben," I said.

"It's Ruby, goddamn it!" he bellowed and slammed down the phone.

Well, it was a lead. Not iron-clad, but it was the first one to show up in three days, if you didn't count being followed by a Bolivian killer the night before.

I checked my watch. Eight-forty. I decided it was too early. I didn't want to case the joint while they were out; I wanted to talk to them.

I turned back to TCM. Barbara Stanwyck was all through solving murders, and Bette Davis was preparing to commit one. I switched to the ESPN channels, looking for a football game. The first four had women's tennis, amateur golf, a basketball game between two junior colleges, and synchronized swimming. I tried a fifth ESPN channel and got a sixty-year-old title fight between Rocky Marciano and Jersey Joe Walcott, and when that was done, a classic battle between Gene Fullmer and Carmen Basilio. They had almost worked up to the Muhammad Ali era when I checked the time again, saw that it was ten-thirty, and decided it was time to go. I didn't want to show up before they got back from dinner or murder or whatever they were out for, but I didn't want to wake them and meet when they were in a foul mood either.

I drove over, decided to park in a cheap lot two blocks away rather than use the valet service and pay parking *and* a tip. I knew the hotel didn't hand out room numbers to anyone who walked up and asked, but I'd faced that problem many times in the past and there was always an easy way around it.

I saw a young man climbing out of a Nick's Pizza car and stopped him on his way into an office building. I asked him if he'd like to make a quick ten dollars, he said sure, and I told him to walk up to the Cincinnatian's front desk and tell them he had a pizza for Joe Smith. If they offered to take it up to him, say no, he had to be paid for it. Once he got the number all he had to do was walk out of sight, count to sixty, and go back out. If they questioned him about still carrying the box, just say the order got mixed up and he'd be back in twenty minutes with the right pizza.

I watched him as he entered. He spent about a minute speaking with the desk clerk, then went to the elevators. Then, just to be safe, he got on one, probably rode it up one floor, counted to sixty, and came back down.

I was waiting for him by his car.

"The room number?" I said.

He smiled and held out his hand. "The ten bucks?"

I gave it to him.

"1723," he said, and walked off to deliver the pizza.

I went into the hotel, walked straight to the elevator, and took it up to the seventeenth floor. There was a middle-aged woman just walking out of room 1718, and I fiddled with a nonexistent shoelace—I gave up shoes with laces years ago—until she was on the elevator and the doors slid shut behind her.

Then I knocked on the door of 1723.

"Who is there?" said a heavily accented voice.

"Room service," I replied.

"We didn't order no room service."

"Compliments of the hotel," I said.

The door opened a few seconds later, and I walked into the room, hands in the air.

"Howdy, gents," I said. "Who's Joe and who's Jim?"

"Paxton!" growled the closer one, pulling a gun out of its shoulder holster.

"I'm not armed," I said. "I'm just here to talk."

The closer guy kept the gun on me while the other walked over and patted me down.

"Clean," he announced.

The gun stayed trained on me.

"Nice room you've got," I said.

"Cut the billshit, Paxton," said the one with the gun.

"That's *bull*shit," I corrected him. "You'll get the hang of the lingo in a few more weeks."

"We ain't staying in this stinking town a few more weeks."

"You know where the money is?" I asked.

They just glared at me.

"Neither do I," I said. "And if we're going to hinder each other, it may very well take a few more weeks than necessary. Now," I added, "which one is which, and no Joe Smith bullshit."

"You go to hell. We are the Smith brothers, and you cannot prove otherwise."

"Okay," I said. "Who's Joe and who's Jim?"

"Just talk, Paxton," said the farther one. "The fact that we haven't killed you yet doesn't mean we won't."

"Okay," I said. "You're looking for the money. I'm looking for the money. Our friend from Chicago is looking for the money. The widow is looking for the money."

"Get to the point."

"The police have your brother in jail. They'll be letting him out, of course, but they know who you are, if not your real names, they know why you're here, and they know what you do for a living. They'll be watching every move you make." I paused in case they had anything to say, but they kept silent. "They know what our friend from Chicago has done, who he works for, and what he's here for, and they're watching him, too." Still no comments. "They know the widow doesn't have the money, they know she wants it, and they'll be watching her too." I stared at them. "I'm the only one they're not watching. If I get the money they think I'll be turning it over to them for a reward. I'm the only one who is free and clear to look for it without police harassment. Am I getting through to you yet?"

"I'll say it once more," said the farther one. "Get to the point."

"The point is if you guys are going to tail me every minute of the day, and the cops are tailing you, they'll know the second I get the money—and believe me, there are a lot more of them than there are of you, and they all have guns. In fact, if you keep following me, I'll just stop looking for it for a year or two. Unlike you, my boss didn't send me to get the money, because I don't have a boss. Am I getting through to you?"

They exchanged glances.

"If you come up with the money and we're *not* following you, how will we know you have it, and how will we get our hands on it?"

"The insurance company is offering a five percent finder's fee," I lied. "Offer me ten percent, and I'm working for you."

"We must discuss it."

"I'll wait," I said.

"With our . . . brother."

"He should be out sometime tomorrow. Will he know where to find you?"

"We have meeting places."

"All right," I said. "We don't know if my phone is bugged, so here's the deal: if you're not on my tail tomorrow or the next day, we have a deal. If I spot you, the deal's off and it's every man for himself." I paused. "And before you think of killing me, just ask yourself who is better equipped to find it: three Bolivians who don't speak the language very well, at least one of whom will be watched by the cops, or a private eye who knows the city inside out and does this kind of thing all the time."

The closer one nodded his head. "You will know tomorrow."

"Fair enough," I said. Then: "Do you mind if I use your john? I had lot to drink at dinner."

They frowned. "John?" said one.

"Bathroom," I replied. "Toilet."

He nodded, and I walked into the bathroom and locked the door. Then I took out the glass and soap dish I'd purchased on the way back from dinner, placed them on the sink, transferred the soap from the old dish to the new, and then wrapped the old glass and dish in Kleenex and stuck them in my coat pocket. I was just about to exit the room when I remembered to flush the toilet so they could hear it.

I walked to the door under their watchful eyes.

"Good night, Joe. Good night, Jim. My best to Sam."

"Shut up," said the closer one.

"Whatever you say," I replied, walking out into the corridor. I made my way to the elevator, and a moment later was walking through the elegant lobby to the front door.

I walked the two blocks to my car, paid the dollar fee for under an hour, which was probably nine bucks less than parking and a tip would have cost at the hotel, and drove straight to police headquarters.

Jim Simmons had gone home, but Bill Calhoun, who'd drawn the night shift this month, was sitting there at the next desk.

"Hi, Eli," he said, looking up. "What can I do for you?"

"Hi, Bill," I said. "I brought you a present."

"Me?" he said, surprised.

"The Cincinnati Police Department," I answered, pulling out the tissue-wrapped glass and dish and placing them on Jim's desk.

"What have we got here?" he asked, standing up and walking over.

"If we're lucky," I said, "if either of the Bolivians had a drink of water or adjusted the soap dish, we'll have some fingerprints so you can find out who they really are. I can't imagine there aren't some warrants out for their arrest, either in Bolivia or somewhere in South America. Once you get an ID, check with Interpol, and maybe we can put these guys on ice until someone with a grudge against them takes 'em off your hands."

"Will do," he promised.

I was feeling pretty pleased with myself when I got home. I could lie to killers just like Sam Spade could lie to Joel Cairo and the Fat Man, and thanks to a brilliant piece of acting I didn't have to look over my shoulder every few minutes while I was hunting for the diamonds.

"Shove over," I said to Marlowe as I plopped down on the couch and hit the remote. "You're dealing with a genius here."

He gave me a look that said: *Okay, genius, what do you know about the diamonds that you didn't know five seconds after Sorrentino told you about them?*

If there is a quicker way to kill a proud, happy, boastful mood than a sober, unimpressed dog that doesn't know he's supposed to worship you, I don't know what it is.

13.

"You did *what*?" demanded Sorrentino as we were sitting across a table from each other, waiting for our beef sandwiches in a Texas Roadhouse toward the center of town.

"I found out where they were staying and I paid them a little visit," I repeated.

"Those guys are *shooters*, Eli! They could have killed you!"

I shook my head. "I walked in with my hands up, I didn't have a gun, and shooting me eliminates the only guy who knows Cincinnati from looking for the diamonds."

"Even so."

"They were never going to shoot me last night." I paused and then smiled. "Today, maybe . . ."

"What the hell did you do?"

I told him.

"And?" he said.

"I heard from Simmons this morning. They got a print off the glass. They should have a name to go with it by tomorrow at the latest. And once they do, he's out of here. And poor old Sam Smith has probably already been given a ticket back to Bolivia."

"Even if you're right, which I doubt, that still leaves one . . . and one is all it takes."

"Fine," I said. "Bolivia has a shooter, I've got one."

He frowned. "I won't risk my life for you, Eli."

"I won't risk mine for you either, if push comes to shove," I told him. "But will you risk it for ten million in diamonds?"

He shrugged. "I don't know. I can't cash 'em in where I'm headed."

"Maybe you won't wind up there," I said. "Save a detective's life and even the scorecard."

Suddenly he grinned. "You make that deal with a lot of enforcers, do you? No wonder you're still alive."

The waitress arrived with our sandwiches.

"Thanks, honey," said Sorrentino. "Can you get me some mustard, please?"

"What kind?" she asked.

"The yellow stuff."

She nodded, walked to another table, picked up a jar, and brought it back to him.

"Thanks," said Sorrentino. Then: "Anyone ever tell you you have beautiful eyes?"

"Not since breakfast," she said in bored tones, heading off to the kitchen.

"I got to work on my timing," he said with a smile.

"And your line, and your manner, and—"

"It works in Chicago," he said defensively.

"They know who you are and who you work for in Chicago," I pointed out.

"Okay, okay," he said. "Now where were we?"

"We were about to figure out our next move," I said. "I think I've gotten our friends from Bolivia off our backs, at least for a while, but we still have to find the diamonds."

"Your fences still haven't heard a thing?"

I shook my head. "When you think about it, it's not exactly surprising. If you stole ten diamonds worth a million apiece, would *you* try to dump them less than a week later?"

"Not in the same town, that's for sure," he said.

"Well, there's your work for the next week," I said. "Check with every fence who's big enough to handle them in every city where your family has connections."

"We've *been* checking on it. We'll keep on checking." He paused. "What about you?"

"Diamonds that valuable, it stands to reason Palanto had them insured," I said. "If I can get a look at the policy, maybe there's something in the description that can help us, or at least alert the fences we're in touch with."

"You think Velma'll give it to you?" he said dubiously.

"Who knows?" I said. "It's worth a try." Suddenly I smiled. "She sure as hell won't give it to *you*."

"That's for goddamned sure," he said, smiling back.

"Okay," I said. "Let's finish our sandwiches and get to work."

"When do we meet next?" he asked.

"Tomorrow for lunch. What do you have a taste for?"

"I know it ain't fancy, but I've kinda developed a taste for this Cincinnati chili," he said. "It's strange, because it isn't really chili at all."

"It's the best junk food ever made. If they'd just called it something else, it'd be in every town in America."

"And it's just here?"

"Here, and a couple of Florida towns where a bunch of Cincinnatians retired to."

"Okay," he said. "I've probably driven past thirty Skyline and Gold Star chili joints. Which one do we meet at?"

"Where are you staying?"

"A Holiday Inn a couple of miles north of here."

He gave me the address.

"There's a Skyline about half a mile up the road from you. Noon?"

"Yeah, that'll be fine."

We finished, he grabbed the check again (not that I reached for it), and then we were on our way, him to keep checking on major out-of-state fences, me to the Grandin Road area.

I almost didn't recognize the Pepperidge Tudor, because for the first time there weren't any cop cars in the driveway. I pulled into the drive, parked, walked up to the door, and rang the buzzer. There was no answer, so I waited a minute and rang again.

Finally the door opened. I half-expected a butler or a maid, but it was Velma herself, wearing a bright-red satin pantsuit.

"*You!*" she hissed.

"Hi, Velma," I said, stepping inside before she could slam the door in my face. "I hope Fluffy's doing well?"

"You don't care about the fucking cat any more than I do."

"Just being polite," I said. "Nice set of widow's weeds."

"We buried the bastard yesterday. How long do you think I have to wear that shit?"

"Do you talk like this to your bridge club, Velma?"

"Just say what you have to say and get the hell out of my house," said Velma. "And it's Mrs. Pepperidge to you."

"All right," I said. "I'm here because we're both after the same thing—the cat's collar."

She stared at me coldly. "It's just a collar. It has a great sentimental value to me."

"It's got great value to just about anyone," I said. "That's what we have to talk about."

She glared at me. "What do you think makes it worth anything to anyone but me?"

"A bunch of twenty-carat diamonds," I said. "How does that stack up against sentimental value?"

She stared at me for another moment, then sighed deeply.

"All right," she said. "Come on in. But wipe your feet first."

I wiped my feet on the rug that was just inside the door.

"This way," she said, leading me to a huge living room, where every piece of furniture and artwork looked like it cost more than a replacement to the Ford would run. "Sit down," she said.

I was about to sit on a beautifully carved chair.

"Not there!" she snapped. "On the couch."

I sat on the couch, sank in a few inches, and waited for her to sit down on a chair that was the littermate to the one I'd been forbidden to touch.

"All right, Piston," she said. "What have you got to say?"

"The first thing I've got to say is that it's Paxton," I replied. "Eli Paxton."

"Get to the point!" she snapped. "I'm a grieving widow."

"The point is that we both want those diamonds recovered," I said. "And with all due respect, I'm probably in a better position to find them than you are."

"Why should I trust you?"

"There are three parties looking for them," I said. "One party consists of three killers from Bolivia. The second is an enforcer from your late husband's Chicago employers. I'm the third." I smiled at her. "Who would you rather trust?"

"None of you," she said.

"So you're going to find them yourself?"

"I might."

"You're the number-one murder suspect, Velma," I said. "You start looking too hard and they're going to conclude that's why you killed him."

"It wasn't me," she half-snapped and half-bellowed. "I loved the bastard!"

"Yeah, I can tell."

"And even if I didn't, he was a source of money. I don't know where he kept it, except for the collar, but whenever I wanted some he gave it to me. Why would I kill him?"

"I don't care if you killed him," I said. "I'm not the police. Try to remember that. I'm just a private eye, trying to focus that eye on some missing diamonds."

"If you think I'll ever let *you* keep them . . ." she began harshly.

I shook my head. "This isn't a game of finders keepers, Velma," I said. "If I keep them, you or the insurance company will charge me with theft, and I won't be able to talk my way out of it."

"With that kind of money you'll hire the kind of lawyers Jim hired and get off scot-free."

"Even Jim's lawyer couldn't prove I had a right to the diamonds," I said. "I just want to find them before the other parties do, and turn them in for a reward."

"Fine," she said. "Go. I'm sick of the sight of you."

"I thought you'd like to make my job easier," I said.

"Fuck you."

"Or at least faster," I continued as Fluffy walked into the room and began rubbing herself against my left leg.

"Oh?" she said, arching an eyebrow.

"I know they're valuable diamonds," I began. "But they aren't the only ones in the world, or even in the Grandin Road area. There's a lot of money within a mile or a mile and a half of here, and probably a lot of diamonds as well."

"So?"

"So if I find them, I need to know if they're the ones that were on the collar," I continued.

She frowned. "How do you do that?"

"Did he buy them after you'd left the mob and moved to Cincinnati?"

"Yes."

"Then they weren't hot," I said. "And if he bought them legitimately, he probably insured them."

"So?"

"So every valuable diamond has an identifying mark, something you need a jeweler's loupe to see. The insurance will describe the marks, so if I come across what looks like the right batch I can make sure of it."

"So you want . . . ?"

"The policy or a copy of it."

"I don't know if he had one."

"Makes sense that he would," I said. "Money was his business."

"But the cat never went out. Well, until . . ."

"But she *could* have darted out," I said. "Or some maid or handyman or anyone else who could spot that the diamonds were real could have taken it off her and left with it. You don't just let ten million dollars go riding around on a cat's neck without some protection—and the most logical protection is an insurance policy."

"Like I said, I don't know if he insured it."

"Has he got an office, a desk, *something*?" I said. "I can check."

"Bullshit!" she snapped, getting to her feet. "You stay right where you are. *I'll* check."

She got up, walked to the staircase, and began climbing up to the second floor, while I spent the next ten minutes petting Fluffy, which I had a feeling was the only thing in the house I was allowed to touch.

She began purring like a buzz saw and didn't climb onto the couch and try to push me off the softest part, which put her one up on Marlowe.

Finally Velma came back down the stairs with a manila envelope in her hand.

"You found it," I said.

"Of course I found it."

I got up, walked over, and reached for it.

"Not so fast!" she snapped.

I looked at her curiously but didn't speak.

"You can make a copy of it. I want the original returned."

"Fair enough," I said.

"If it's not back in ninety minutes, I'm calling the police and telling them that you stole it."

"Have you always been a trusting soul, Velma, or has it just come with . . . ah . . . maturity?"

"Get the fuck out of my sight!" she yelled.

I walked to the door, and Fluffy decided she'd had enough of Velma too. I stooped down, gently pushed her back into the house, and closed the door before she could follow me out.

I got in the car, drove to an office supply shop a couple of miles away, just past Hyde Park Square, made a copy of the policy, and was back at Velma's place twenty minutes later. I rang the bell, and same as last time I waited a minute and then rang it again. Clearly she'd either fired the help or given them the week off to celebrate Big Jim Palanto's unfortunate demise.

The door cracked open.

"Don't come in," she said. "Just hand me the policy."

I passed the envelope over to her.

"I'll be in touch," I said.

"Not until you get the fucking diamonds," she said and slammed the door shut.

I decided, driving home, that I envied Big Jim. Not the money, not the lifestyle, but the fact that he'd never have to see his Velma again.

14.

I actually made it to my bed and spent the whole night fighting Marlowe for the pillow, which was annoying as all hell because I knew that if I'd fallen asleep for the night in front of the TV I'd have been fighting him for the softest cushion on the couch.

I woke up when Bettie Page, who had miraculously morphed into Marlowe half a second earlier, sneezed in my ear, and since my watch, which I'd forgotten to remove as usual, said it was 9:30, I figured I might as well stay up. Marlowe figured so too and started prancing nervously while I climbed into those few clothes—my shirt, my tie, and one sock—that I hadn't slept in and raced me to the door.

"Yeah, yeah," I said. "I know. You gotta go first."

So I clipped the leash onto his collar, tried to ignore my own bladder, and took him out for a walk. This time he didn't even make it to Mrs. Garabaldi's, which was fine with me, since it was drizzling again. As soon as he was done pretending to be a lawn sprinkler I turned around and headed for home.

Mrs. Cominsky was waiting for me.

"It's working!" she announced excitedly.

"The furnace?" I said. "I hadn't noticed that it had stopped again."

"No!" she said. "Our ruse!"

"Which ruse was that?" I asked, still half-asleep.

She pointed to a huge box of mail. "Our ad! There was so much that the mailman left it in one of the post office's white plastic boxes."

"Look, it wasn't the best idea I ever had," I said. "Counting today's mail, and what's doubtless coming tomorrow, we've got hundreds of people who swear they found the cat and turned it in, and would like their reward."

"Oh," she said, frowning. "I hadn't considered that."

And suddenly I saw a way to simplify my life for a few days.

"Still," I continued, "there's always a chance that one of them has made a telltale blunder. As long as we're partners in this little enterprise, why don't you give them a first run-through and then pass on any that look truly suspicious?"

"I'll get on it right after I do the laundry!" she promised.

"Good," I said.

"Great!" she said. "Gonna catch us a cat thief, we are!"

"Let's hope so," I said, walking past her and climbing the stairs with Marlowe. When we got inside he explained to me that his food bowl was empty, so I opened the fridge, pulled out a couple of not-quite-stale jelly donuts, and tossed them in his bowl.

Then, while he was growling at and terrorizing the donuts prior to eating them, I finally made it to the bathroom and pulled out the insurance policy to see if it made any more sense in the daylight than it had the night before. Oh, there was no question that Palanto—well, Pepperidge—had taken it out, and no doubt it was for ten diamonds. It was dated three years ago, and that made sense too, since he'd been retired when he'd moved to Cincinnati, probably started working for the Bolivian drug lords seven or eight years ago, and hadn't started siphoning off money until three or four years back.

But after that it got confusing. If Sorrentino's information was correct, he should have been sitting on ten million dollars' worth of diamonds . . . but the policy was for only *one* million.

That didn't make sense. If they were worth ten million and you were going on record as insuring them, why insure them for just 10 percent of their value? And if they were only worth a million and you were worth, I don't know, maybe thirty or forty million, why insure them at all?

My only conclusion was that it was some tax dodge I didn't understand, not having been a multi-millionaire in this particular lifetime, and I made up my mind to talk to an accountant about it later.

The other thing that baffled me was the description of the diamonds. Not the *actual* description—so many centimeters, so many grams, so many carats—but the *technical* description, with terms and symbols that looked like some alien language. I don't mean French or German; I mean Martian or Saturnian.

I read the thing through a few more times, realized I had to meet Sorrentino for lunch before long, and headed out.

I got to the Skyline Chili joint a couple of minutes ahead of him, ordered a coffee, and wished newspapers were still worth reading so I'd have something to do besides stare at the other diners. Finally Sorrentino showed up, walked over, and took a seat.

"Anything?" he asked.

"Yeah," I said. "I got the insurance policy from Velma yesterday."

"She *gave* it to you?"

"Unhappily, but eventually of her own free will," I replied.

"Anything interesting in it?"

I nodded. "I thought you told me that the diamonds were worth ten million."

"Yeah," replied Sorrentino.

I frowned. "Then why did he only insure them for one million?"

"That's gotta be wrong."

"I just read the damned policy twenty minutes ago," I said.

"My first thought is that he did it to throw potential thieves off," said Sorrentino. "But that's crazy. If it's one million or ten million, it's still worth stealing. And who the hell was going to look at the insurance policy first? A good guess is that no one except Velma and his insurance agent ever saw it."

"Okay," I said. "I'm open to suggestions."

"The best suggestion I've got is that it's a typo."

"Come on, Val," I said. "Even if it *is* a typo, don't you think Palanto or his agent would notice in three years' time that all his payments were based on a one-million-dollar policy?"

He shrugged and displayed his hands, palms up. "You got me."

He was about to say something else when the teenaged waitress came by. He glanced at the menu and frowned. "I love this stuff, but three-way, four-way, five-way, what the hell's the difference?"

"Try 'em all and decide which you prefer."

"Hopefully I ain't gonna be in town that long," he answered.

"C'mon, mister," said the waitress. "I got other customers, y'know."

"Okay," said Sorrentino, jerking a thumb in my direction. "I'll have what he's having."

She turned to me and even stopped chewing her gum for a minute.

"I'll have a four-way," I said.

"Me, too," Sorrentino chimed in as she was walking away from the table.

We sat in silence for almost three minutes until she returned with the food.

"Damn it, Eli, Palanto wasn't lying!" he half-shouted, startling the other diners. "I'd bet everything I have on that."

"I believe you," I said. "I just don't know if I believe *him*."

"Everyone else does," he said.

I shook my head. "Who the hell is 'everyone'? The Bolivians are here for the money he siphoned off, but to this minute they don't know anything about the cat or its collar. If they'd killed him and they knew about it, they'd have removed the collar, and if the cat got by them and they thought it might jump, they'd have shot it. I mean, hell, if they'd already killed Palanto, how much more trouble could they be in for killing a cat?"

He sighed heavily. "I know."

"And as for Velma, whether it was worth ten million or one million, there's no way she'd be acting any differently. It's loaded with diamonds, they're probably legally *her* diamonds now unless we can prove he stole them, and from everything you've told me about her, and all that I've experienced myself, she'd have had them arrest me if the diamonds were only worth a thousand apiece."

He stared at me for a long moment. "You're ruining my meal," he said at last.

"Finally, there's you," I said.

"Me?"

I nodded. "I think you've been straight with me, but even if you haven't, would you have gone back to Chicago if the diamonds were only worth a million?"

"You think I've been lying to you all along?" he said in hurt tones.

"No, Val, I don't," I answered. "I'm just pointing out that even if the diamonds were only worth a million, or even half a million, no one would be behaving any differently."

He sighed. "All right, all right. Now let me finish this stuff in peace." He dug into his four-way. "Whoever heard of chili with shredded cheese and spaghetti?"

"You're the one who wanted a Cincinnati chili joint," I pointed out.

He chewed his mouthful thoughtfully and swallowed. "I can't imagine why this stuff hasn't caught on."

"Ask yourself if any self-respecting Chicago restaurant owner would open a Cincinnati chili place."

He considered it for a moment. "You got a point," he admitted. Then: "Okay, we're friends again. What's our next step?"

"Well, I have to check in with the cops and see if the print on the glass was any use to them. And I have to figure out why Palanto lied to you. I mean, was he just trying to impress you, and if he was, wouldn't a million-dollar collar be as impressive as a ten-million-dollar collar?"

"That's a fair day's work."

"Oh, there's more," I said.

"Yeah?"

I nodded. "I got to figure out what the hell those descriptions on the policy meant."

"I don't follow you," said Sorrentino.

"There have got to be more hot diamonds in town than just the ones stolen from the collar," I explained. "If one of my fences comes up with some, or one of my snitches tells me where some are, I have to make sure they're the right ones."

"Shit!" he said. "I never thought of that."

"And if the print wasn't any good, or if it was good but they can't deport the Smith brothers anyway . . ."

"They sound like cough drops."

"Yeah, but I'll bet they don't *shoot* like cough drops."

"Okay," he said. "Where do we meet for dinner?"

I named a local steak house as he finished the last of his four-way and washed it down with a Pepsi.

"See you then," he said.

"Right."

"And let me say that the last sixty seconds have been a real eye-opener."

"They have?" I asked, puzzled.

He nodded. "I always knew there were good reasons never to become a cop or a private eye. You just reminded me of some of the better ones."

15.

Mrs. Cominsky was waiting for me when I got home.

"Hi, partner!" she said.

"Hi, partner," I responded somewhat less enthusiastically.

"Ain't you gonna ask?" she said.

"Ask what?"

"About the mail!"

"Okay," I said. "What about the mail?"

"I've gone through about three hundred already."

"Anything worth reporting?" I asked, hoping to get the charade over with before some other tenant stumbled upon us talking "business" in the entryway.

"More than two hundred out-and-out liars, maybe forty perverts, six religious fanatics, two insurance salesmen, a writer who wanted to buy you lunch and get the rights to the heartwarming story of your reunion with the cat, and the rest were mostly animals lovers who congratulated you on getting the cat back, and I think at least a dozen of them want you to breed your cat to their cat and split the litter, though no one seemed to know what sex your cat is."

"And you still have more to go," I noted with a smile.

"They could come in three or four hundred a day for a week," she replied. "But *somebody* is going to make a mistake, I'll pounce on it, and we'll have our man."

"Right," I said, remembering a couple of bad paperbacks I'd read recently. "A good cop just keeps on plugging away—and that goes double for private eyes."

She was quiet for a moment. Then: "How much does a license cost?"

"Car or cat?" I asked.

She shook her head impatiently. "A private eye's license. Once we crack this case, maybe I'll apply for one. This is the most interesting thing I've done in years."

I resisted the urge to ask her what was the *least* interesting thing she'd done in years.

"I like your attitude, partner," I said. "Just keep at it. When you come to The Letter That Counts, let me know—or if I'm out, slip a message under the door." *And if you spill a little gravy on it, Marlowe will be your friend forever, once he recovers from digesting it.*

"Will do, partner!" she said enthusiastically. "I had no idea reading mail from liars and perverts could be so interesting."

"After a few years, it'll feel like reading the classified ads in the paper," I assured her.

"The thrill wears off, huh?"

"Well, maybe not for really special detectives," I said.

"That's me!" she said. "I'd stay and chat, but . . ."

"I know. Go open them, and good luck."

I finally climbed the stairs, unlocked the door, said hello to Marlowe (who growled hello to me and went back to sleep), walked over to the section of the couch he'd left me, sat down, and started reading the insurance policy again. It didn't make a lot of sense this time either.

I kept coming back to the insured value. Even if the company's jewelry appraiser was dead wrong, why would Palanto have paid for the policy when he knew the diamonds were worth ten times as much?

And if they *weren't* worth ten times as much, where the hell was the other money that he'd scammed from the Bolivians? It wasn't in his bank account, the cops had gotten permission to check his safety deposit box, and Velma had to know every hiding place he had in the house and garage.

And I kept coming to the same conclusions. The Bolivians would have been fools to kill him unless they had their hands on the money or knew where it was . . . and it was clear from the fact that they were still hanging around that they didn't know. And it was just as obvious

Velma figured all the money was in those ten diamonds. But that didn't make sense. She had access to the insurance policy and had me arrested because she thought I'd stolen the collar. If she knew the collar was worth 10 percent of what Palanto was hiding *somewhere*—and if she knew where it was, she'd be getting a new name and face in some other state or country.

I continued to stare at the policy.

"If you'd only been for ten million, this fucking case would make a hell of a lot more sense," I muttered.

Shut up when someone's trying to sleep, growled Marlowe, stretching his feet as he lay on his side and digging his nails into my thigh.

I picked up the remote and turned on the TV. There weren't any basketball games on for a few more hours. The best ESPN could do was a rerun of the fourth Pacquiao-Marquez fight, and I'd already lost enough money betting on it the first time. I tried TCM, hoping for something with Bogart or maybe with the team of Greenstreet and Lorre, who I persisted in thinking of as the Mutt and Jeff of international crime, but instead they were having a John Garfield festival. I watched the second half of *The Postman Always Rings Twice* and the first ten minutes of *Saturday's Children*, trying all the time not to think about the diamonds, and finally I couldn't sit still any longer. I turned off the set, forced Marlowe to go for a walk while I tried to clear my head, let him make a beeline for the couch when we got back, stuffed the insurance form into my coat pocket, and went back out.

I don't know one jeweler from another (well, except for the fences, those who'll talk to me and those who won't), but I figured if I stayed within a mile or two of Palanto's house I couldn't go too far wrong. So I drove over to his place, then hunted up the nearest upscale shopping area, and stopped at Kaiser's Jewelers.

The window looked impressive. I'd seen enough bullet-proof glass to know I was looking at some, and the prices on the stuff that was displayed there justified the expenditure for the glass and doubtless for one hell of an alarm system as well.

At the moment there was one middle-aged woman there, looking at watches or watchbands, I couldn't tell which, and since I needed the jeweler's attention I lit up a cigarette—only my second of the day (well, if you don't count the two I snubbed out after only a couple of puffs), found myself staring into a lingerie shop and attracting giggles from a couple of teenaged girls who were passing by, and moved on to pretend to be studying "Authentic! Oriental!! Rugs!!!" in the next store. I was starting to get really cold just standing there, so I only smoked half the cigarette, stamped on its remains and shoved it into a gutter, and walked into the jewelry store just as the lady was leaving.

"Good afternoon," said the jeweler, a balding little man with thick glasses. "May I help you?"

"I certainly hope so," I replied. "I have to tell you up front that I'm not here to buy anything. You're way out of my price range. I'm a detective, working on a case, and I need some information."

He gave me a little smile. "That woman who just left took up half an hour of my time for the third time this week. She's not going to buy anything either, but she hasn't even admitted it to herself, let alone to me. So why can't I take a few minutes educating an officer of the law?"

It's been my experience that half the people think I'm an ugly version of Humphrey Bogart, and the other half think I work for the police—and since I was taking up this guy's time for free I decided not to correct his wrong impression.

"Fine," I said. "My name is Eli Paxton."

He extended a hand, and I took it. "And I am Phineas Kaiser. Now, what can I do for you, Mr. Paxton—or is it Officer Paxton?"

"Just Eli will do," I said. I pulled the policy out of my pocket and handed it to him.

"It looks like an insurance policy," he said.

"It is. It's for ten diamonds, and they average one hundred thousand dollars apiece."

He nodded, looking the policy over. "Nice tidy sum. They must be quite beautiful, these diamonds."

"I've never seen them," I said.

Suddenly his face lit up. "Hah! They've been stolen!"

"In all likelihood," I replied.

"In all likelihood?" he repeated. "You're a detective, you've never seen them, you're showing me the policy. Of course they've been stolen."

"Stolen or well-hidden by their owner."

"Why not ask him if he hid them? Or is this some insurance scam?"

"It gets really complex," I said. "Anyway, I need some information, and an expert opinion."

"You've come to the right place," he said. "Well, one of them anyway. What exactly do you need to know?"

"The policy describes each diamond," I said. "How it was cut, how many carats, any flaws, just about everything there is to know about them."

He nodded, studying the policy. "That's correct. Very thorough job."

"Okay," I said. "Here's my first question: does that seem like a fair appraisal of their worth?"

"The Bateman Company has been insuring jewels as far north as Cleveland and as far south as Nashville for half a century," he replied. "Have you some reason to think they were mistaken?"

I shrugged. "I've no idea."

He smiled. "Of course you have an idea, or you wouldn't have asked. How much do *you* think they're worth?"

"I don't know anything about diamonds, so my opinion would be meaningless," I said. "But *someone* thinks they might be worth a lot more than a million dollars."

"How much more?" asked Kaiser.

"Maybe ten million?" I said, feeling like a fool.

He laughed. "Based on this description, on their size and weight and color, not a chance. Maybe a million and a half in an up market, but surely no more than that." He glanced down at the policy. "Three years old," he noted. "Prices haven't varied five percent since then."

"You're sure?" I said.

He drew himself up to his full, if minimal, height. "I know my trade, Mr. Paxton."

"Eli," I corrected him.

"Have you any other questions?"

I thought about it for a moment. "Yeah, one more," I said. "I've been assuming that if these things turn up, it'll be with a fence."

He smiled. "If you want the names and addresses of all the fences in the Tri-State area, I think your department is far better informed than I am."

"No, I don't need their names," I said. "But it occurs to me that they might not go through a fence. I mean, someone who can steal a million dollars' worth of diamonds can probably find a way to prove they're his if no one looks too closely."

"I don't think I like what you're suggesting," said Kaiser.

"I'm not suggesting that anyone could dupe *you*, especially now that we've had this conversation," I said. "I'm just blue-skying here, wondering if someone with some kind of forged ownership credentials might try to unload them on a legitimate jeweler, or on a number of legit jewelers."

He frowned. "I don't know, Mr. Paxton . . . Eli. He'd be taking quite a chance that someone could spot phony ownership papers. Fences won't care, so why take the chance?"

"You don't deal with fences, I take it?"

"Of course not," he said severely.

"If you thought you had a wealthy customer who was about to buy his girlfriend a truly splendid diamond engagement ring, and you thought one of these diamonds might be just what he was looking for, and you know you could charge him a million for the diamond, plus whatever the setting and your time are worth, what would you pay me for the diamond if I could prove to your, shall we say, eager satisfaction, that I was the legitimate owner?"

"I'd have to consider the ring, the work required . . ." Kaiser began.

"If you knew it was a sure sale for more than a hundred grand, would you pay ninety?" I asked. "Eighty-eight?"

He thought about it for a moment, then nodded. "Probably. But I'd have to be sure at both ends—that my customer was willing and able to pay for it, and that you were the true owner."

"So you'd pay ninety percent of the diamond's value for a legitimate sale?" I said.

"If the other conditions were as stated," replied Kaiser.

I gave him a huge grin. "You know what a fence will pay for a hot diamond?"

"I have no idea," he answered.

"Between five and ten percent, depending on how hot it is and how long he has to keep it off the market. Now do you know why I'm thinking that maybe the diamonds might show up at a respectable diamond merchant's like this one?"

"I see!" he said, wide-eyed with wonderment. Suddenly he laughed. "Clearly I should have been a fence!"

"Stay legit," I said. "You deal with a better class of clientele. Safer, anyway."

"Sound advice," replied Kaiser. Then: "Have you any other questions?"

"Just one. You got a Xerox machine?"

"A photocopier? Yes."

"Then make a copy of the descriptions and keep it handy."

"You could just leave the policy here," he suggested.

I shook my head. "No, I've got to make a copy for every jeweler in the area. Hell, probably in the county."

"Ah, yes," he said. "I see. Well, hand me the policy, I'll copy the essential parts in the back room, and return it in less than a minute." He took the policy to his office or work room or whatever it was, and was back almost instantly.

"You know," he said, returning the papers to me, "I could just call all the other dealers—the ones who can handle this kind of transaction—and have them contact you if and when someone tries to unload the hundred-thousand-dollar diamonds."

I shook my head. "Ain't gonna happen."

"I don't follow you," he said, frowning.

"There'll be some jewelers who might not be as careful as they should with a one-hundred-thousand-dollar diamond," I said, "but any jeweler who's confronted by ten of them is going to make dead sure of the identity of the seller at the very least. If I were a betting man, and I am, I'd make it even money that if someone tries to unload them at all, they'll be spread over half a dozen shops."

"I see," he said. Then: "You've got your work cut out for you, Eli. You don't even know for a fact that they'll try to sell them here, or that they're still in the city."

"Oh, they're in the city," I said.

"How can you be sure?"

"Because every person who would kill for them is still in the city," I answered.

He stared at me for a long moment. "You make me very happy that I'm just a jeweler," he said at last.

16.

Imet Sorrentino for dinner. He hadn't learned a damned thing, and neither had I. The cow that supplied the steak had been a muscle builder that would put Arnold Schwarzenegger to shame. Dessert wasn't much better, and we agreed to meet at yet another Bob Evans for lunch the next day. Then I remembered that it was Sunday, and I had planned to stay home and watch the Bengals, so we agreed to skip lunch and meet at a German joint, of which Cincinnati has its share, for dinner.

I was really looking forward to kicking off my shoes, fighting Marlowe for the couch cushion that was directly in front of the TV, and watching Cary Grant portray Cary Grant in a quartet of movies.

But before I could unlock the door to my apartment, Mrs. Cominsky rushed up to me.

"Three hundred and seventy-two more, just today," she announced.

"Find the guilty party yet?" I asked without much interest.

"Guilty of *what*?" she responded. "We've got seven for-sure rapists, a dozen sodomists, nine pedophiles, twenty-two hookers . . . and the list goes on and on."

"The charm of living in the city," I said, forcing a smile.

"Makes me afraid to walk to the supermarket," she said.

"Well, turn 'em over to the cops and let *them* worry about it," I said, trying unsuccessfully to get by her and put my key in the lock.

"Not yet," she said quickly. "There are some I need to study further."

"To see who returned the cat?"

She looked blank for a moment, and then my question registered. "Oh, of course," she said quickly. "Definitely. That's what this is all about."

"Right," I said. Marlowe, who had doubtless been listening, finally barked, now that the dirty parts were over. "If you'll excuse me, I'd better take the dog for a walk before he does something dreadful to your rug."

"My *carpet!*" she snapped.

She stepped aside as I unlocked and opened the door. Marlowe was standing just on the other side, and his expression seemed to ask why I was wasting my time with this dirty old lady when I could be walking him in the freezing rain. I didn't have an answer, so I stuck a leash on him and took him outside.

He'd just finished blessing Mrs. Garabaldi's petunias in his own unique way when she stuck her head out the window and began cursing us both out, as usual.

"Hey, Mrs. Garabaldi," I said. "I want to make amends for my dog's poor behavior." She stared at me, frowning. "Mrs. Cominsky down the street has a bunch of pornographic letters she'd like to share with you."

She kept staring.

"I'm not kidding. They're the real thing."

"Mrs. Cominsky?" she said at last.

"Right."

"Dirty letters?"

"Filthy," I said.

She closed the window without another word. I went straight home and never did see if she showed up or not, but the thought of the two old biddies poring over those letters kept me warm on a chilly winter night.

The next day, I woke up half an hour before kickoff, watched the Bengals almost blow a twenty-point lead, met Sorrentino for dinner, exchanged three pleasantries and no information, and went back home, where Marlowe and I spent a few hours watching Gary Cooper say "Yup" and "Nope" and occasionally shoot the bad guys. I walked him one more time and went to bed.

This time I was photographing Bettie Page on a beach. There was no one within miles of the two of us, and she was twenty-four years old again. I told her I loved her. She opened her moist red lips to answer, and nothing came out but a ringing sound.

"Bettie, are you all right?" I said apprehensively.

She smiled reassuringly and tried to tell me she was fine and madly in love with me, but she made that ringing noise again.

Suddenly the wind growled in my ear. It seemed to be saying, *Answer the fucking telephone.*

I sat up in the bed, shook my head a couple of times to remove Bettie from it, told Marlowe to shut the hell up, and picked up the phone.

"Hello?" I muttered.

"Mr. Paxton?"

"Right," I said, blinking my eyes to get some of the sleep out of them.

"This is Phineas Kaiser."

"Who?" I said groggily.

"Phineas Kaiser."

"Do I know you?"

"I'm a jeweler. You were in my store on Saturday."

"Oh! Right!" I said, suddenly alert. "What can I do for you, Mr. Kaiser?"

"Nothing," he replied. "But perhaps *I* can do something for *you.*"

"I'm all ears."

"I passed the word about your missing diamonds to some of my colleagues, the ones who might expect to handle such items. And I scanned the insurance policy's description and e-mailed it to them."

"And?" I said, trying to keep my excitement out of my voice.

"And Winslow Monroe, who runs a shop about a mile from mine, tells me he was offered a diamond ring that was worth in the neighborhood of one hundred thousand dollars. He passed on it—even a jeweler of Winslow's stature doesn't shell out that kind of money without a buyer in mind—and he returned it to her. But of course he examined it very thoroughly, and he is certain it was one of your missing diamonds."

"And his name is Winslow Monroe?" I said.

"That's correct."

"Do you happen to have his address?"

He gave it to me. I'd fallen asleep in my pants and shirt, so I pulled a pen out of my pocket. I couldn't find any paper on the bed table, so I wrote it down on my shirt cuff.

"Thanks, Mr. Kaiser," I said. "What time does he open?"

"It's eleven o'clock," answered Kaiser. "He's been open for two hours."

"You've been a big help," I said. "If there's ever anything I can do to thank you, just let me know."

"Well . . ." he began slowly.

"Yes?"

"Next time you're near the store, please drop in and inspect my burglar alarm system. I've been wondering if it's time to update it."

"You got yourself a deal, Mr. Kaiser," I promised him.

We hung up, I decided to change shirts, and then Marlowe reminded me that it was time to walk the dog. I took him out, and even though he spread more holy water on Mrs. Garabaldi's petunias, there was no cursing.

"Eli," I muttered to myself as we turned to go back home, "you've made two old ladies very happy."

I decided that it was my good deed for the month, and it was time to get back to work. I returned Marlowe to the apartment, barely avoided him as he made a dash for the couch, and went off to talk diamonds with the one man who had actually seen what I was looking for.

17.

Winslow Monroe's shop was called The Pearl Diver, which at least was attention-getting. So was the stuff he had on display in his window—the usual rings and bracelets and necklaces, but also a golden sword with rubies and emeralds embedded in the handle, and a beautifully carved cuckoo clock that was perpetually open at three o'clock, showing an onyx bird with diamond eyes and a sapphire beak poised to squawk out the hour.

I walked in, pretended to browse while a young guy argued about the price of a ring, and watched while he stormed out of the place.

Winslow Monroe, a middle-aged man with a neat little mustache and goatee, looked at me and shrugged apologetically.

"I'm sorry for that gentleman's behavior," he said. "How may I help you?"

"You can start by not calling him a gentleman so I'll know I can trust your judgment on other things," I said.

He chuckled. "I stand corrected."

"My name is Eli Paxton," I began.

"Ah, yes!" he said. "My friend Phineas told me to expect you. Would you like some coffee? I have some brewing in the workshop."

"I would love some coffee," I assured him.

He put a "Closed—Back in 20 Minutes" sign on the front door, locked it, and led me through to what I would have called a cross between a back office and a storage room, but there *was* a table filled with a number of delicate instruments I'd never seen before.

"Have a seat, Mr. Paxton," he said, indicating a stool.

"Thanks," I replied, taking off my coat and hanging it on a hook on the wall, then sitting down next to a work table.

"Cream? Sugar?"

"Whatever makes you happy," I replied.

"I prefer mine black."

"Then black's fine by me," I said. "What I care about is the caffeine."

He smiled. "Yes, I imagine you must keep some rather strange hours in your profession."

"And I imagine you must handle some interesting objects in yours," I replied as he carried two cups to the bench, set one down in front of me, and sat down opposite me.

"Probably less than you would think or I had feared when I got into this profession and opened this store," he replied. "Cincinnati is not exactly a haven for master criminals."

"It's got its share," I replied, taking a sip of the coffee. "Which is what I'm here to talk about."

He nodded. "Yes, Phineas faxed me the policy. He wanted to scan and e-mail it, but I'm not very comfortable around computers."

"Welcome to the club," I said.

"Anyway, based on the excellent description of the diamonds—size, weight, cut, color, coding—I am convinced that I saw one of the stones you're looking for."

"Mr. Kaiser said it was in a ring?"

He nodded. "A young woman—very pretty, looked to be in her midtwenties, brought it in and asked me what it was worth. I told her that in my professional opinion it would bring perhaps ninety thousand dollars at a legitimate auction, but that very few jewelers would give her anywhere near that much unless they had a customer waiting for just such an item, and I, alas, did not."

"And that was it?" I asked. "She didn't say who gave it to her, how she came by it?"

"May I be blunt, and perhaps a tad vulgar?" he replied.

"Yeah, I think I can stand it," I said with a smile.

"Her clothes looked like they were from off the rack at Walmart, her shoes were much the same quality, and I couldn't help but notice that she drove up in a car that was"—he paused, considering his next words carefully—"almost as old as yours." He took a long sip of his coffee. "It is my considered opinion that women like that do not buy or inherit such jewelry."

"I'm not inclined to argue with you," I answered.

"Now, Phineas said there were ten stones. I have not seen the other nine."

"At least now I know one's still in the area," I said. "That's more than I knew yesterday." Then came the money question. "Do you have her name and any contact information?"

He nodded. "She left it with me, in case a buyer materialized in the next few days, though I gather she planned to keep trying to sell it elsewhere."

"She's still got it," I said with conviction.

"What makes you think so?"

"It hasn't turned up with any of the bigger fences, and I would assume every jeweler who can afford it has your reluctance to buy it without a customer in the offering."

"True," he said, nodding his agreement. "And there's one more thing as well."

"Let me guess," I said, finishing my coffee.

"Go ahead."

"No legitimate jeweler's going to shell out even half what it's worth without proof of ownership, and if she got it the way we both think she got it, that's one thing I'm pretty sure she can't supply."

He smiled. "Phineas said you were good at your job."

I grimaced. "If I was good at my job, I'd know who stole the damned collar, and then I'd know who the killer was."

"I beg your pardon?" he said, startled.

"Just detective talk," I said. "Pay no attention."

"There was a murder?"

"There was a murder."

"Let me guess," he said. "Malcolm Pepperidge?"

I nodded. "Was he a customer?"

He shook his head. "No. I heard about his murder on the radio a few days ago." He paused. "A fine, upstanding citizen from everything I've heard about him."

"Yeah, that's what they say," I responded.

"And you've been hired to catch the killer?"

"No, that's the cops' job."

"Then shouldn't they be looking for the diamonds too?" he asked.

"They will eventually," I said.

He frowned. "Why not now?"

"There's some possibility that they weren't stolen," I answered.

"Then you think Pepperidge gave the ring to . . . ?" He let the sentence hang there.

"It's a possibility," I said.

And it was. In fact, every time I encountered her it was more and more difficult to believe a man with Palanto's money and background didn't have a girl on the side, maybe two or three.

"That's a mighty big diamond to give to a girlfriend, but I suppose when you're as wealthy as Malcolm Pepperidge . . ." He finished his coffee. "Did you know there was a rumor that he was considering bringing the Royals—or at least some NBA team—back to Cincinnati?"

"They're before my time," I said. "I'm not a native, though of course I've heard about them."

"They were really something," he said, his face lighting up. "I was just a kid, but I remember the Big O."

"Oscar Robertson?" I asked.

He nodded. "They traded him, and two years later they were gone. The city never forgave them. I had real hopes for Mr. Pepperidge."

I decided not to disillusion him. But if Palanto was sitting on eighty million dollars and they gave him the stadium for free, that money might buy a two-year contract with a LeBron James or Kobe Bryant, but he'd still have to find a way to pay the other eleven players and the coach. As rich as he was, he was no billionaire, and owning a pro sports franchise was a billionaire's game.

I looked at my wristwatch. "You've been closed for fifteen minutes,"

I said. "I don't want to cost you any business, so if you'll just give me the girl's name and contact info, I'll be on my way."

"Right," he agreed.

He got up and walked over to a small desk, fumbled through a pile of papers, pulled one out, copied it down on a fresh sheet, and handed it to me.

I took it from him and read it aloud: "Mitzi Cramer." I looked up. "Mitzi? There hasn't been a Mitzi since Mitzi Gaynor."

"Who was she?" he asked.

"See what I mean?" I continued reading. "Hell, she lives a couple of miles west of me. Pepperidge could have gotten her for a much smaller diamond."

"I wonder what she was doing in this area?" he mused.

"Looking for a better price."

He considered my answer, then nodded his agreement. "Yes, I suppose so."

"Well," I said, standing up, "I don't want to take up any more of your time."

"Actually, I've enjoyed our conversation immensely," he said, getting up and walking me to the door, where he took down the "Closed" sign. "I love my work. There's nothing I'd rather do. But excitement doesn't exactly go with the job."

"Unless you're robbed," I said.

"Please!" he responded. "Don't even joke about it!"

"I apologize."

"Happily accepted," he said. "If any more of the diamonds turn up, I'll contact you. Phineas gave me your number."

"I appreciate it," I said, shaking his hand and heading out into the street.

I wondered if I had time to get across town and hunt up Mitzi Cramer before I had to meet Sorrentino for lunch. I decided since I didn't plan to share anything I learned with him until we turned in the diamonds, I figured I couldn't tell him what I didn't know. So I stopped by the apartment, took Marlowe for a walk, and waved to Mrs. Garabaldi, who looked like she was about to blow me a kiss but exercised remarkable self-restraint. Then I headed off to Bob Evans to lie to my partner.

18.

Sorrentino didn't have anything to report, and I didn't have anything I *wanted* to report, so we had a pleasant meal, talked about the Bengals and the Bears, couldn't decide whether Muhammad Ali in his prime could have beaten Mike Tyson in his, and mostly settled for enjoying our sandwiches and coffee.

He had a few calls in to his bosses' West Coast fences and was in no hurry to leave since they rarely got in to work before noon their time, but I wanted to get over to the West Side and hunt up the lady with the ring.

While we were waiting for the check, he decided he wanted to debate whether Zenyatta could have beaten Ruffian at nine furlongs, and that turned into whether Affirmed was better than Alydar or just luckier. Finally I made an excuse that I had to visit the men's room, stayed there seven minutes by my watch, and when I emerged he had paid the bill and was waiting by the door.

"You okay?" he asked.

I nodded. "Forgot to shave. Just taking care of it."

He studied me. "You missed a few spots."

"They give me character," I replied.

"Nuzzle a girl and you're gonna have more than character," he said with a smile. "You're gonna have one hell of a slap in the face."

"I'll only nuzzle girls with beards," I said.

"What about dinner?"

"Nice Mediterranean joint opened up a few months ago." I gave him the address.

"What's Mediterranean?"

"Like Greek, only different." I told him how to get there.

He grimaced. "Thanks a lot. Seven o'clock?"

"Sounds good," I said, walking out the door before he could start another conversation.

I got to the Ford, had a little trouble starting it up but finally managed, and headed off to the west. I slowed down when I got within a few blocks of my destination and surveyed the area. Nice, well-kept apartment buildings, probably built in the 1940s and 1950s. (Someone once told me when I was considering moving to Cincinnati that if I wanted to see what America was like during Eisenhower's presidency, come to Cincinnati. And of course Mark Twain once remarked that if the world came to an end, he wanted to be in Cincinnati because everything happens five years later here.)

It was a nice enough neighborhood. Little shops on the corners, tiny but well-manicured lawns. To hear the locals describe the town, Interstate 75 is the north-south running dividing line, and all the money is on the east side. Well, most of it is, but that doesn't mean everything west of the highway is a slum. It's very nice, just not, well, Grandin Road nice.

I pulled up to the address I'd been given, got out of the car, waited for a kid on a skateboard to coast down the sidewalk, entered the building, and went to the row of doorbells, looking for one with Mitzi Cramer's name on it.

I rang, waited for an answering buzz to let me in, but none was forthcoming. I tried twice more with no response. I couldn't believe that a girl who was walking around with a hundred grand on her finger was working a nine-to-five job, especially given what Winslow Monroe had suggested, so I went back to the car, climbed into it, tried to find a station that wasn't playing rock music, finally got some twenty-four-hour news channel, and got a quick education in Ethiopia's latest hunger crisis.

I'd been there about an hour when the most gorgeous blonde I'd seen since coming to Cincinnati a few years ago came walking—well, undulating—down the street. Her skirt wasn't *that* short, her heels weren't *that* high, despite the cold she was just starting to open her coat and her neckline wasn't *that* low, but you took one look and knew she'd be a unanimous choice for Playmate of the Year, even if, like Zenyatta, she had to give weight to all her overmatched competitors.

I didn't need a second look to know that this was Mitzi Cramer. I checked her hand and there it was, glistening in the afternoon sun.

I was afraid if I stopped her on the street she might make a scene, so I waited for her to go into her building, gave her time to climb the stairs to wherever her apartment was, and then got out of the door, entered the building, and rang her bell again.

The building wasn't new enough—or perhaps the landlord wasn't generous enough—to have an answering system so the person could call down and ask who was there. You either pressed the buzzer and let your guest in or you didn't . . . and since based on what Monroe had told me she was unlikely to turn callers away, I wasn't surprised when the buzzer sounded and the inner door unlocked.

I climbed a flight of stairs, didn't see any open doors, then climbed up to the third floor. A door was cracked open, and a blue eye peeked out.

"Do I know you?" she asked.

"Not yet, Mitzi," I said, pulling out my detective's license and holding it up for her to see. "I'd like to talk to you."

"I've stayed clean," she said defensively.

"I'm sure you have," I said. "May I come in? It won't take long."

She stared at me. "I don't know."

"We can talk here or down at the station," I lied. "It's up to you."

That did the trick. She opened the door, stepped aside as I entered, and then led me to a living room that was furnished a little better than the average.

"Have a seat, Mister . . . ?"

"Paxton," I said, sitting on a chair rather than a sofa so she wouldn't feel she had to sit on the same piece of furniture. "Eli Paxton."

She sat down, facing me. "What do you want?"

"You can tell me who gave you that ring," I said.

She covered the ring with her free hand.

"Why?" she demanded.

"It has to do with a case I'm working on."

"I don't know what you think I done for it . . ." she began.

"Mitzi, I don't *care* what you did for it. I just want to know who gave it to you."

She stared at the ring, then looked up at me. "It's hot, right?"

"That depends on who gave it to you," I said. "Give me the right name and you can keep it for all I give a damn. Give me the wrong name and it's potential evidence in a—" I decided not to use the word *murder* "—criminal case."

Her entire body relaxed, which was eye-popping in its own way. "Okay," she said, clearly relieved. "It was a gift from a very wealthy gentleman friend from the other side of town. He's got all kinds of connections and was going to help me become an actress."

Shit! I thought. *Palanto gave it to her, he had every right to, and we're back where we started.*

"Sounds good," I said. "Just for the record, what was his name?"

"Abner," she replied. "Abner Delahunt."

I frowned. "Abner Delahunt?" I repeated. "I've never heard of him."

"Why would you?" she said. "He's a big real estate tycoon, and surely you ain't investigating *him*. I mean, he could afford a dozen rings like this."

"I suppose so," I agreed. "But he won't be giving you another, will he?"

"What are you talking about?" she demanded.

"How do you think I found you, Mitzi?"

She just stared at me without saying anything.

"I got your address from a jeweler you tried to sell it to," I told her. "That doesn't sound like a girl who expects her sugar daddy to keep her in diamonds, does it?"

For a minute I thought she was going to throw a lamp at me. Then all the tension went out of her body, and she just leaned back on the sofa.

"We split up," she said at last.

"Less than a week after he gave you the ring?"

"How did you know that? It didn't come from that jeweler, that Mister . . ."

"Monroe," I said.

"Right, Monroe. My gentleman friend didn't buy it from him, so how do you know when I got it?"

"It's only been missing about a week."

"The ring?" she demanded. "But my initials are on it!"

"Not the ring," I answered. "The diamond."

"But he doesn't have to steal nothing!" she protested. "He's a millionaire! He lives in a great big mansion over there in Hyde Park!"

"I'm not saying *he* stole it," I replied gently. "I'm saying that *someone* stole it, and he wound up with it."

That didn't sound good even to *me*. If he could afford that kind of stone, why the hell was he dealing in a hot one? Sure, maybe he had a wife who was being kept in the dark about Mitzi, but how did a hot stone that the cops would soon be after make it any darker?

"Just a minute," she said. "If it wasn't even a ring a week ago, what makes you think it was stolen?"

"The diamond was insured." I kept it singular; why tell her there were nine more missing? "The insurance policy describes it in such detail that any competent jeweler could identify it, and you took it to one whose shop is just a mile or so from Delahunt."

"Well, believe me, he's loaded," she said. "He wouldn't have to steal the damned thing. He could buy it with his pocket change. Probably some deadbeat sold it to him for cash and then put in a phony claim with the insurance company."

"That's not the way it happened," I said. "This is serious business, Mitzi. You're almost certainly going to be called to testify before it's over."

"Testify that a gentleman friend gave me a present?" she said. "Like it's never happened before?"

"It's never happened in quite these circumstances," I answered.

Then I figured I might as well shoot for the moon. "Tell me, Mitzi, did your friend—"

"Ex-friend," she interrupted me.

"My mistake. Did your ex-friend Abner come into possession of a cat at about the time he gave you the ring?"

"How the hell would I know?" she shot back.

"He didn't mention it?" I said. "Nothing about a cat?"

"No," she said adamantly. "Are you going to accuse him of being a cat thief as well?"

It'd sure make life easy if I could, I thought.

"No, it's just something very peripherally related to the case."

She glared at me and finally spoke: "I hate cops."

"I'm not a cop," I said. "I'm private."

"Big difference," she snorted. "I hate you too." She paused. "You working for the insurance company?"

Since I didn't know who the hell I was working for—Velma, myself, the Chicago mob—I nodded my head and told her that she was right.

"Figures," she said. "Maybe Abner should have bought an insurance company along with all that other stuff."

"Can I ask why you broke up with him?"

"I didn't."

I frowned. "I thought you just told me—"

"You think I'd break up with a man the same week he gave me a sparkler like this?" she said, holding her hand out so the light hit the diamond. "I ain't that kind of girl."

"So *he* broke up with *you*?" I said. "The same week he gave you the diamond. Why?"

"His wife was sniffing around. She knew he was seeing someone, but she didn't know it was me." She shrugged, which too was eye-popping. "How the hell could she? We've never met, and he had enough brains not to leave my number lying around the house." She grimaced. "So he said we couldn't see each other for half a year or so, until the coast was clear, and then we'd go off to live on an island in the Pacific." Another grimace. "I've heard that kind of shit before, although not from anyone who could afford it until Abner showed up. But I could tell he never planned to see me again, or if he did, it was going to be even more on the sly, just a bunch of wham-bam-thank-you-ma'am nights. I figured hell, the ring ain't hardly an emotional keepsake under those circumstances, so I might as well sell it and pay some bills, get some new clothes, maybe take a trip to the Big Apple and start auditioning."

"Not to LA?" I asked. "A girl with your looks?"

"Hollywood is loaded with girls with my looks," she said with the kind of smile men kill for. "We're a little rarer in New York."

"Would you happen to have his address?"

She gave it to me, and I scribbled it down in my notebook.

"He's not much to look at," she said. "Small, kind of chubby, going bald. But he can be a really sweet guy."

"I'm sure he can," I said. "One last question: Where did you meet him?"

"At the Shoe."

"The Horseshoe Casino?"

She nodded. "I'm attracted to big plungers. They don't have to win. I mean, hell, no one wins all the time. But if they can afford to make big bets, the odds are they're good for it."

"Makes sense to me," I said. My own limit was five dollars at the Shoe and ten at River Downs.

"Anyway, Abner was a plunger. Or he was when I met him. He didn't mind being seen with me at first, but for the past few months we stayed away from the Shoe. I think he was afraid some friend or maybe even a relative might spot us."

I got to my feet. "Thank you for your cooperation, Mitzi."

"And I can keep the ring?"

"For the time being," I said. "If you can't, someone else—someone a lot more official than me—will be by to pick it up." I paused. "In the meantime, I'd appreciate it if you didn't tell Abner I was here." Why let him know anyone was on his trail until we'd amassed enough evidence to nail him?

"I won't be talking to him again, and he sure as hell ain't calling me," she said. "Hell, I just might take an extended vacation."

I shook my head. "I can't stop you, but I wouldn't advise it. If what you've told me is true, you are innocent of any of the crimes connected with the diamond."

"Crimes?" she interrupted.

"It's very complex," I answered. "Anyway, I'd advise you to remain innocent. You leave town, and I can almost guarantee there'll be a warrant out for your arrest in a day or two. Innocent is the best policy."

She walked over and gave me a hug. She felt as good as she looked and smelled even better.

"What was that all about?" I asked when she stepped back.

She smiled at me. "It's been a long time since anyone said I was innocent."

I chuckled, walked out the door, and was driving back to my apartment a minute later. When I arrived I was just about to unlock my door when I became aware of the fact that I wasn't alone.

"Good afternoon, Mrs. Cominsky."

"I've been reading mail all afternoon," she said. "I'm afraid to go outside."

"You think you'll run into the mailman bringing another load?"

She frowned. "Don't be fallacious."

"You mean facetious?" I asked.

"Whatever." She looked around, but there were no perverts hiding in the second-floor corridor. "This town is filled with liars and sex maniacs!"

"And that comes as a surprise to you?"

"Have you *read* these things, Mr. Paxton?"

"No. You've got 'em all."

"I'll give you some of the filthiest ones."

"I shock easily," I said. "You keep 'em."

"Well, I did give some to that nice Mrs. Garabaldi. She said you told her I needed help going through them." She paused. "We spent an hour today exchanging the most outrageous ones."

"I don't suppose you've figured out who found and returned the cat yet?"

"Cat?" she said. "What cat?"

"The object of the exercise," I said.

"Oh! The cat" she said, suddenly nodding. "I'm working on it."

"Well, keep at it," I said.

"Oh, I will," she promised. "I will."

She marched off—I almost said "toddled off," but she hadn't toddled in thirty years—and I opened the door.

Go away, said Marlowe, opening one eye.

I got the leash. "Come on," I said. "I know your bladder is stronger than mine, but even you need a walk now and then."

He growled but let me put the leash on him. A freezing rain started to fall the instant we were outside, and three minutes later we were back. As I was kicking off my shoes the phone rang.

"Yeah?"

"Hi, Eli," said Jim Simmons. "I've been trying to reach you all afternoon."

"What's up?"

"We traced your Joe Smith fingerprint."

"Unless it was Jim Smith," I said. "What did you come up with?"

"His name is Tupak Morales, and he's wanted in seven different South American countries, five of them for murder." He paused. "We owe you, pal. You found us a big one."

"Have you picked him up yet?"

"He and his partner are out grabbing a late lunch or early dinner now," answered Simmons. "We're tailing them, and thanks to you we know where they're staying, and we'll pick him up tonight."

"So with a little luck, you can deport them all in chains, or at least cuffs, in a day or two?"

"Two of them for sure," he answered. "The one we've already got and Tupak. I'll be surprised if the other hasn't also got warrants out for his arrest all over the hemisphere."

"Good," I said. "Glad I was able to get that print." Then a thought occurred to me. "Uh, Jim . . ."

"Yeah?"

"On the off-chance that you have nothing on the third, or that this Tupak character can somehow make bail, I'd appreciate it if you didn't tell him how you identified him."

"You got it, Eli."

"Well, that solves one problem, anyway," I said, hanging up.

Marlowe stared at me as I walked over to sit on that portion of the couch he'd left for me.

You don't really think it's going to be this easy, do you? he said, and somehow I knew he wasn't talking about taking back my couch cushion.

19.

I met Sorrentino at seven. He spent fifteen minutes trying to decipher the menu into known dishes. (Hell, I say that as if I'm some kind of sophisticate. I didn't know what they were either, but given the prices—he was still paying—I figured all the dishes must be pretty good, so I just picked the one that sounded the best when I tried to pronounce it.)

"So," he said, "any progress?"

"Not much," I lied. "Spoke to a couple of minor-league fences, but they hadn't heard anything. And you?"

He shook his head. "They haven't shown up on either coast, or in Chicago or Miami."

"I *do* have some news," I said, feeling I had to toss him something before he got too suspicious.

"Oh?"

I nodded. "They've identified two of the Smith brothers," I replied. "They should be on their way back to Bolivia, in cuffs, in a day or two."

"And the third?" he asked.

"They're working on it."

"That makes us two-thirds safer, but it doesn't get us any closer to the damned diamonds," he said. "If I didn't know from other sources—my friends in Chicago—that he really did swipe millions from them, I'd say our info was wrong and all he had was a million . . . but damn it, *he* said he had ten million on the collar, my organization says he skimmed between ten and thirteen mil off the Bolivians, and I can't imagine they'd send three hit men here for less. So why the hell were they only insured for a million?"

I smiled. "That was the longest speech you've made since we met."

"It's driving me crazy!" he said. "I *know* he skimmed at least ten million! He himself admitted it. It's not in any account he had access to, and we both know if it was in a safety deposit box or somewhere else where Velma could get her hands on it, she'd have grabbed it and blown town five minutes later."

"It's probably with whoever killed him," I suggested.

He considered it, then shook his head. "Ten diamonds worth maybe a million bucks. Where's the rest of it?"

"That's what we're being paid to find out," I said, and then smiled. "Except that nobody's paying us, at least not until we find it."

The main course arrived, and we stopped talking and dug in.

"Not bad," said Sorrentino after a couple of bites. "What's yours like?"

I shrugged. "Beats the hell out of me. Some kind of meat in some kind of sauce, with some kind of vegetables and bread mixed in. Damned good. And yours?"

"Mostly fish," he said. "I think." He paused a moment. "Good, though."

We concentrated on eating, were too full for dessert, and made arrangements to meet at a burger joint at noon. He picked up the tab, and we went out to our cars.

I assume he went back to his hotel. Me, I drove down to police headquarters and hunted up Bill Calhoun. I figured I needed to know a little more about Delahunt before I confronted him.

"You're too late if you're looking for Simmons," he said when he saw me.

"You'll do just as well," I said.

"Uh-oh!" he said. "The last time I did just as well, I wound up with two guys shooting at me."

"Ancient history," I said, since it had happened almost four months ago. "I don't need you to leave the office for this one."

He stared at me suspiciously. "Spell it out, Eli."

"I want you to turn on your computer and hunt up some information for me."

"If it's confidential you'll have to get—"

"Who said anything about confidential?" I interrupted. "I just need you to pull up some stuff."

"There's Jim's computer," he said, pointing at the machine on Simmons's desk.

"I see it."

"So sit down and hunt up your info," said Calhoun.

"I can't," I said.

"Why the hell not?"

"I don't know how to work a computer."

He sighed deeply. "No cell phone. No GPS. Yeah, it figures." He started typing on his own machine. "Okay, what do you need?"

"Anything you can find on Abner Delahunt."

"Delahunt?" he repeated. "Isn't he that real estate mogul? Got offices all over the East Side of city?"

I nodded. "That's the one."

"Well, let's see what Wiki has to say about him, if anything."

"Who's Wiki?" I asked.

He shot me a look of pure pity. "*Wikipedia*," he replied. "It's an online encyclopedia."

"I don't know if he's done anything to merit being in an encyclopedia."

Another similar look. "You'd be surprised at who's in *Wikipedia*." He began typing. "Yeah, here he is: Abner Delahunt, age fifty-six, married to Lorraine, two children, both grown and out of the house. He's got degrees from Cornell and Stanford." Calhoun frowned. "Both coasts. I wonder how he wound up in Cincinnati? He's a little too young for 'Nam and too old for Iraq, but he helped bring Truth, Justice, and the American Way to Granada." He paused as more information came up on the screen. "Went into real estate in the eighties, seems to have made a couple of fortunes, big donor to his church and the Republican Party." He stopped typing and looked up. "Sounds like a good upstanding Cincinnatian."

"Anything's possible," I said.

"You didn't ask me to look him up if you didn't think there was some kind of problem with him."

"There may be," I said.

"Well?" he said. "What kind?"

"I don't know. That's why I'm asking you."

He grimaced. "It would help if you'd tell me what the hell you're looking for."

"I wish I knew," I said. "Just anything out of the ordinary."

"Well, let's see if he's ever been arrested for anything."

"Wiki-whatever has stuff like that for the general public?" I asked, surprised.

He chuckled. "No. But this is a police computer." He began typing. "No, never been arrested." Suddenly he frowned. "Now, *that's* curious."

"What is?"

"He's got a couple of lawsuits pending against his organization."

"His real estate company?" I asked.

He nodded. "Yeah."

"Who's suing?"

"One of his landlords," said Calhoun, bringing up more information on the screen. "Seems he's way behind on his rent on . . . let me see . . . seven of his offices. And it looks like he's written a couple of bouncers on a pair of leased cars, a Mercedes and a Lincoln." He shrugged. "So much for being a tycoon."

"Is that information up to date?" I asked.

"Within a week or two, I'd say." He stared at me. "Does the guy owe you money?"

"No."

"You're grinning like the cat that ate the canary."

"Am I?" I said.

"May I assume Mr. Delahunt is the canary?"

"Could be," I said. "How long do you plan to be here, Bill?"

"I started at eight tonight. I'll be knocking off at four-thirty, unless Bob Hess oversleeps again."

I shook my head. "Not long enough."

"Not long enough for what?"

"Tell you what," I said. "Either leave Jim Simmons a note or check it out yourself when you show up tomorrow . . . but I'll bet that information you just gave me is out of date."

"You think he owes more?"

"I think he's paid them all off."

"Yeah?" he said, arching an eyebrow. "And why do you think so?"

"I'll tell you when I *know* so," I replied. "Thanks for your help."

Before he could ask me any more questions I was heading to my car, and fifteen minutes later I was walking Marlowe over to Mrs. Garabaldi's petunias.

"Yeah, Asta," I said to him. "I think we cracked the case, and I don't even have a Nora."

He looked at me, and his expression seemed to say: *I ain't Asta, you ain't Nick, Nora left you years ago, and nothing's as easy as you think it's going to be.*

20.

I got up at nine, walked Marlowe, opened a can of Campbell's chicken noodle soup for him, paused in the hall long enough for Mrs. Cominsky to explain that these letters were too filthy for our good, upright, honorable police force to read, and that she'd be keeping them safe and sound against the day of Final Retribution. When I gently suggested that Final Retribution rested with a higher power, she assured me that she had gone to church and told God exactly where to look for the letters.

Once away from the apartment, I got into the car and drove over to Hyde Park and started doing a little checking.

The first thing I found was that Delahunt had put his house up for sale four months ago—and had taken it off the market three days ago.

I asked a couple of rival realtors about his empire. They admitted that he'd been Mister Big in luxury real estate properties for quite a few years, but the current economy had hurt him more than most. He'd already closed four offices in the less affluent areas, and he was losing staff in some of the others, not that anyone was buying them off, but that the word being whispered on the street was that even when they made a rare sale of a million-dollar property, he was late paying his agents' commissions.

It sure as hell sounds like a mogul who was going broke until this week . . . and the only things that had changed were that his friend Malcolm Pepperidge was dead and he seemed to have an influx of money.

I ate a quick, noncommittal lunch with Sorrentino, then went back to Delahunt's home turf. His private golf club told me he'd let his membership lapse but had called them this week to say he'd be renewing it when spring rolled around. The local Republicans assumed he hadn't made any donations in the past year because he didn't like their candidates, but of course he was loyal to the core Republicans.

Every place I checked and every answer I got led me to the same conclusion: he was a formerly wealthy man who'd been hurting for cash for a couple of years and was suddenly, in the past few days, starting to drag his fallen credit rating back up by its bootstraps.

By midafternoon I'd done enough checking. I went home, popped open a beer, poured another into Marlowe's empty food bowl, turned on one of the lesser ESPN channels, and watched some girls in and almost out of bikinis play beach volleyball for a wildly enthusiastic audience who probably didn't even know the rules and certainly didn't know the participants' names. If you were a breast man you cheered for the girl on the left; if you were a leg man you cheered for the one on the right. If you liked them both, as I did, then you were a nonpartisan.

The game ended, they switched to bowling, and I switched to reading a secondhand paperback I'd bought at a local Book Nook, in which the hard-boiled hero shot a bad guy in odd-numbered chapters and bedded one or more women who looked even better than Mitzi Cramer in the even-numbered ones.

Finally it was about half an hour before I was due to have dinner with Sorrentino. I considered taking Marlowe for another walk, but as I approached him he looked up from his couch cushion and gave me one of his *don't you dare come hither* looks, so I walked to the car, almost bumped into Mrs. Garabaldi as she was coming over to discuss very current literature—like this morning's—with Mrs. Cominsky, and twenty minutes later I parked a couple of blocks from the Montgomery Inn, which specialized in ribs, celebrities, and Reds and Bengals jerseys—the ribs were for eating, the others for being impressed by.

Sorrentino was already there, and we were soon seated at a table.

"How'd your day go?" I asked.

"Same as the last few," he said grimly. "Zip. How about you?"

I decided I couldn't hide what I knew any longer. If there was one guy besides the Brazilians I didn't want mad at me, I was sitting across the table from him.

"I'm pretty sure I know who killed Palanto," I said.

He leaned forward. "Tell me about it."

"I've been doing some detective work," I said. "I didn't want to say anything before I had something concrete."

"And now you do?"

"I think so."

"Well?"

"I managed to trace one of the diamonds," I said.

"Where is it?" he asked.

"In a ring on the finger of a girl who makes Pam Anderson look like a boy."

He nodded his head thoughtfully. "Isn't it always? So was Palanto her sugar daddy? Did she knock him off?"

"No," I said. "I doubt that she ever met him."

"Okay," said Sorrentino. "So who killed him?"

"There's a guy, Abner Delahunt, who lives three doors down from Palanto," I replied. "A guess is that just about everyone on that street belonged to the same golf club and probably the same church. The guy was a realtor, had a dozen offices around town . . . but he fell on hard times, had to close a few of them, hadn't been paying his bills. Looked for sure like he was about to go down the drain."

"And he's been paying them since Palanto's death?" asked Sorrentino.

I nodded. "And the girl's only had the ring a few days."

"Sounds good to me," he said. "Why the hell didn't you fill me in while you were tracking all this info down?"

"I know what you did to those kids who jumped you the other day," I said. "Just in case this was a bad lead or a dead end, I didn't want you getting rough with the girl. I'd have had to testify, and you're my friend. I didn't want you going to jail for nothing."

Suddenly a grin spread across his face. "And you didn't want me beating you to the diamonds."

"That, too," I admitted, returning his grin.

"Well, what the hell, what you have sounds good. What's our next step?"

"We pay him a visit," I said. "If we send the cops there and he's got any of the diamonds left, they'll confiscate them and there goes our reward."

"Makes sense," he agreed. "Let's go now."

"And miss the best rib dinner in the country?" I said. "Don't worry. The blonde's not going to warn him."

"What makes you so sure?"

"Because she knows if we nail him, her ring's evidence. She's probably hoping I'll go after someone else, or that Delahunt will buy me off."

"Or kill you."

"I don't think it'd bother her a bit," I said as the waiter came by and I gave him my order. Sorrentino, who hadn't looked at the menu, just said, "The same," and a few minutes later we were gorging ourselves on two slabs of ribs.

When we were done we walked out onto the street, and Sorrentino turned to me.

"I assume we're going there to make, if not a citizen's arrest, a citizen's search, authorized or otherwise?"

"We'll play it by ear," I said. "But remember: if we search the place without permission, we probably won't be allowed to keep what we find long enough to turn it over to the insurance company."

He patted the slight bulge under the arm of his sports jacket. "Oh, I think they'll give us permission."

"Just follow my lead and don't threaten anyone," I said.

"So how the hell are we going to do this legally?"

"Theoretically I'm working for Velma," I answered. "If I claim that you're my assistant, and we've been tipped that the murder weapon is there and we'd like permission to do a quick search for it, I'm sure that's the one thing that's so well hidden, if it's on the premises at all, that Delahunt will give us the okay and plan to trash the damned gun tomorrow if he hasn't already. And once we have permission to search the place, then if we find the diamonds, we should be in the clear for turning them in."

"I hear a lot of 'ifs,'" said Sorrentino.

"If you've got a better plan, tell me now so if there's anything illegal I can point it out."

"No, we'll play it your way."

"Okay," I said, reaching my car. "Follow me. We'll park a few blocks away, and then you can get in my car."

"Why?" he asked.

"You're supposed to be my assistant. It makes sense that we'd arrive together."

He nodded. "Okay."

We got into our cars, I drove down Interstate 71 to the Dana Road exit, went a little less than a mile to Edwards, turned right, and a couple of minutes later we passed by Palanto's house. Delahunt's was three houses down the street, and I could see that there was no "For Sale" sign on it. I drove another block, parked, waited for Sorrentino to park behind me and climb into my car, and then I circled around and parked in the street in front of Delahunt's huge Tudor.

"Something wrong with the driveway?" asked Sorrentino.

"I'm making two assumptions," I replied. "One, that Delahunt is a murderer, and two, that he operated alone. If I'm wrong about the first, it'll be embarrassing as hell, but no real harm done ... but if I'm wrong about the second, I don't want his accomplice to trap us in the driveway."

He smiled. "I got to start thinking more like a cop."

"A shamus," I said. "If they still use that term."

"Only in old Bogey movies, I think."

We got out of the car and walked up the winding flagstone path to the front door. I touched the bell and heard chimes suddenly play the opening notes of "Hail, Hail, the Gang's All Here." A moment later a middle-aged woman wearing a maid's outfit opened the door, and even in the dim light I could tell that she had a lousy dye job.

"May I help you?" she asked.

"We'd like to see Mr. Delahunt," I said.

"I'm afraid he's not here."

"Is Mrs. Delahunt at home?" I asked. If the maid was alone, I'd already decided to show her my license, which everyone seems to think makes me a cop, and tell her we had a search warrant.

"I'll get her," she said. She stood stock-still, as if trying to decide whether to shut the door in our faces until she could hunt up her boss. "Won't you please come in?" she said at last.

"Thank you," I said, and Sorrentino and I stepped into the large tiled foyer.

A moment later an elegant woman of perhaps fifty approached us. She wasn't pretty, but she sure as hell was as handsome as money, grooming, and bearing could make her.

"You wish to see me?" she said by way of greeting.

"Yes, ma'am," I said. "My name is Eli Paxton, and this is my assistant, Mr. Sorrentino." I flashed my license. "We came here to see your husband, but I wonder if we might ask you a couple of questions."

"What is this about?" she demanded.

"I'll get right to the point," I said. "This is an inquiry into the whereabouts of a certain diamond, about which we believe Mr. Delahunt may have some information."

"I *knew* it!" she exploded. "That stupid son of a bitch!"

"I beg your pardon?" I said, genuinely surprised.

"Him and that damned bimbo of his!"

"Are you perhaps referring to a Miss Cramer?" I asked.

"I don't know her name!" she spat. "But I know that we're down to one car and one servant, and we're probably going to have to move to a smaller place, but he's got enough money to give a diamond to that blonde bitch! He thought I didn't overhear her thanking him for it on the phone!"

"Are you fully aware of what you're saying, ma'am?" I asked.

"Hell, I'll say it in court! I'm leaving that bastard! He can have the bimbo *and* the diamond, and I hope they'll keep him warm in his goddamned jail cell!"

Sorrentino and I exchanged looks. Each said the same thing: *I do believe we're in business.*

21.

She gave us permission to search the house. Not many people are as good at tossing a room or a house as I am, but Sorrentino was one of them. We found a lot of stuff that didn't belong in the house of a wealthy, happily married business tycoon—love letters from a pair of girlfriends hidden in one of his business folders in a desk drawer, a warning from the electric company that they'd be cutting off his service if he didn't bring his bill up to date, dunning letters from half a dozen stores and creditors, all of them relatively recent. I turned the love letters over to his wife to thank her for her help and to give her a little extra ammunition against him.

But when we'd finished two hours later there were two things that we hadn't found—the diamonds and anything that might conceivably have been the murder weapon. Mrs. Delahunt was almost as disappointed as we were and told us we had carte blanche to come back, alone or with the cops, whenever we wanted. I asked where her husband was, but all she could answer was: "In one of his offices that hasn't been shut down yet, or with one of his whores who hasn't been shut down yet. I don't know and I don't care."

I dropped Sorrentino by his car, and he followed me to a bar in Clifton, the university area, about four miles away. We both parked on the street, tried not to feel too ancient as we made our way past all the late teens and early twenty-somethings standing at the long bar, and took a table as far from the noise as we could get.

"Well, what do you think?" he asked as we waited for the bearded waiter to approach us.

"We've probably got enough for Simmons to arrest him, especially with his wife on our side," I said. "But with no gun and no diamonds . . ." I just shook my head. "He'd be lawyered up and out the next morning. Always assuming he has enough money to hire a lawyer."

"I don't give a shit about that," said Sorrentino. "I'm not a cop, and neither are you. What about the diamonds?"

I shrugged. "He sure as hell doesn't have them in the house. If he's hiding them, we have to figure out where. If he sold them—and he has to have sold at least *some* of them, since none of his creditors have taken him to court yet—we have to figure out who he sold them to."

"Okay," he said. "Our next step is easy enough. I get him alone and beat the shit out of him until he talks."

I shook my head. "This isn't Chicago, Val," I said. "The cops won't look the other way. You beat the information out of him, at worst you'll be up for battery, at best the cops will claim you were trying to steal the diamonds and you'll lose all claim to a finder's fee."

He frowned. "Then what do *you* suggest?"

"We keep trying to find the diamonds," I said. "They're what we're after. If we don't have any contact with Delahunt, no one can claim bribery, extortion, intimidation, or anything else."

"Your cops would actually do that?" he asked.

"Absolutely. Like I say, this isn't Chicago."

He shook his head in wonderment. "Strange city."

"We'll look for the gun, too," I added.

"Why do we care?" replied Sorrentino. "All we want is the god-damned diamonds."

"We find the diamonds and you're in Chicago a few hours later. But I'll be staying in Cincinnati with a very bitter man who's already killed someone with that gun and who will be convinced that I'm the only reason he couldn't stop his life from going down the tubes."

"I hadn't thought of that," he admitted.

I smiled. "Why should you? You're going to be safe and sound three hundred miles away."

"Okay, okay," he said. "So what about the diamonds?"

"I think if he'd left them with any of the Cincinnati fences I'd know by now, and while I haven't spoken to Simmons I'm sure he has a man on the job too," I said. "So I have a feeling we're going to need your organization's connections to find them. We'll keep looking here, of course, and I think it might make sense for us to take turns keeping an eye on Delahunt, but I really don't know what else we can do."

"You think his wife knows anything?"

I shook my head. "She's so mad at him, she'd be first in line to tell us anything that would put him away for life."

"Yeah. I suppose so," he agreed. "Well, my people aren't without their resources. I can find out within, say, forty-eight hours how much he's got in the bank. I can probably even find out if he's visited a safety deposit box. He must have one; there was no safe in the house. And of course we can check his business accounts too."

And suddenly, as he was speaking, I began to get an idea. Maybe it would amount to nothing, but we were running out of approaches. And if I was right, I'd have to do it alone.

We talked a little more, wound up comparing the Big Red Machine to the 1959 White Sox, and Walter Payton's Bears to Boomer Esiason's Bengals, and finally we finished our beers and walked out to where we'd left the cars.

"So where do we meet for lunch?" he asked.

I knew it would have to be within a few minutes of the river, so I thought for a moment and answered, "Joe's Diner, over on Sycamore Street."

He laughed. "Come on, Eli. Where are we really meeting?"

"I just told you: Joe's Diner. You've got a Global Whatever. You'll find it."

"There's actually a place called Joe's Diner?"

"It's a landmark," I told him.

He snorted. "Is there anything in this town that *isn't* a landmark?"

"Not much," I answered.

"Okay. Noon?"

"Make it one o'clock," I said. "I'm running a little short on sleep, and I don't want you waiting alone at a table for half an hour. Hell, you might get so bored you decide to run off with Mrs. Delahunt."

He grimaced. "Okay, one o'clock."

He climbed into his car, and a moment later I did the same. I'd bought myself maybe three and a half hours before lunch tomorrow. I hoped it was enough time.

22.

When I left the bar I waited until Sorrentino was out of sight, then drove straight to police headquarters. Jim Simmons had gone home for the night, but Bill Calhoun was there, and I walked over and sat down opposite him at his desk.

"You know, Eli," he said, "you really ought to learn to use a computer one of these days."

"I'm a detective, not a typist," I said.

"Well, I'm a police officer, not a typist—but I know how to work a computer."

"Good!" I said. "Then you're just the man I want."

He signed deeply. "Okay, okay, what do you need this time?"

"The guy you hunted up for me . . ." I began.

"Delahunt?"

"Yeah."

"What about him?" asked Calhoun.

"I got to thinking," I said. "He's got a bunch of real estate offices."

"*Had* a bunch," Calhoun corrected me. "Most of them are closed now."

"I know. But they're all in Cincinnati, right?"

"Right," he said, looking at me curiously.

"His house—hell, the whole Grandin Road area—can't be more than five or six miles from the river, right?"

He frowned. "Yeah, I'd say six miles, tops."

"And half the Reds and Bengals live just across the Ohio River in Kentucky because it's convenient for them to get to the stadiums, so there's got to be some expensive real estate there," I continued.

"Yeah, I suppose there is."

"So does he have any offices there?"

"There?" repeated Calhoun. "You mean in Kentucky?"

I nodded. "Right."

"So what if he does?"

"So what I'm looking for may not be in Ohio," I answered.

"You know, you could just look in a Northern Kentucky yellow pages," he said.

"If that was all I needed, I'd look," I said. "Now, are you going to help a tax-paying citizen or not?"

"When did you ever make enough to pay taxes?" he shot back, but he began typing and studying his screen.

"Yeah, he's got an office in Covington, on Third Street. Looks like a big one."

"How can you tell it's a big one?" I asked.

He smiled. "Three phone numbers."

"Any other offices across the river?"

He typed again. "No. He had one two years ago, but he closed it about twenty months ago."

"Okay," I said. "Now I need you to do something that won't show up in your system."

He stared at me, frowning. "Eli, everything I do from this office shows up *somewhere* in the system sooner or later."

"Damn!" I muttered.

"What was it?" he asked. "Maybe there's a work-around."

"I need to know if he's got a bank account, either personal or business, in Kentucky."

"I can check on the bank account, but I can't keep it secret."

"How about a safety deposit box?"

He shook his head. "I can call the bank, identify myself, and ask, but there's no way I can do it with my computer, and they'll probably tell him about the call five minutes later."

"Oh, well," I said unhappily. "If push comes to shove, I'll get my friend from Chicago to find out."

"The guy who showed up the night we brought in the first Bolivian? I heard he was connected to you somehow. Can he really do that?"

"*He* can't," I replied. "But his people can."

"I believe it." Calhoun leaned back. "Anything else I can do for our favorite public-minded citizen?"

"Anything else your machine can tell me about Delahunt?"

"Probably not, but I'll look," said Calhoun, starting to type again. "Why are you so interested in him?"

"The truth?" I said. "He may have killed Malcolm Pepperidge."

He turned to me. "That's a hell of an accusation. Have you told Jim?"

"Jim doesn't care about 'may haves.' He wants proof. I'm trying to get it."

"Have you got any yet?"

"Not a shred," I said. "That's what you're helping me to find."

"From what I hear, Pepperidge wasn't interested in real estate."

"Pepperidge wasn't even Pepperidge," I said.

"Yeah, I heard that too."

"So can you give me anything else on Delahunt?"

"Go outside and have a cigarette—don't deny it; everyone knows you smoke—and give me five or ten minutes to work without having to talk to you."

I walked out to the parking area, lit up a cigarette, took a deep drag, closed my eyes, and leaned against a brick wall, trying to relax, then took another puff. I smoked it halfway down, tossed it on the ground and stepped on it, lit another, and repeated the process. When I felt I'd frozen my ass off for ten minutes, I went back to Calhoun's desk.

"Well?" I asked.

"Not much," he said.

"What?"

"Just one thing," he said. "That diminishing real estate empire of his was incorporated in Kentucky."

"Why?"

He shrugged. "Better tax structure. It does seem to be the one office that was never late on its rent."

"How many employees?"

"In Kentucky?" He shrugged. "No way to tell."

"Okay," I said. "Thanks, Bill."

"I don't know quite what I've found," said Calhoun, "but I hope it helps."

"You and me both," I said, heading out of the building. I got into the car, started it up, and headed for home.

Marlowe was snoring so loud I could hear him through the door as I inserted my key and entered the apartment.

He gave me a hurt, angry look that said, *You went out for dinner and then you went out drinking, and you didn't bring me any food or any booze.* Before I could mollify him he was asleep again.

I set the alarm for eight o'clock, then decided I wasn't as sleepy as I'd thought. I walked to the living room, fought Marlowe for a little space on the couch, and turned on Turner Classic Movies just in time to see Orson Welles say "Rosebud!" I decided I'd rather watch some sports and got a sixty-year-old kinescope of a welterweight match between Kid Gavilán and Chuck Davey, a college student who had no business being in the ring with the likes of the Kid except that he was white, personable, and lacked a sense of self-preservation.

When that was over they began showing a kinescope of Rocky Marciano dismantling Ezzard Charles. I fell asleep in the third round and woke up when Marlowe began barking an inch from my right ear, just in case I didn't hear the alarm ringing.

I dragged myself to the bathroom, shaved, brushed my teeth, considered changing shirts and decided against it, then wandered into the kitchen. I opened a can of hash for Marlowe, grabbed a stale donut and a cup of coffee for myself, then decided I'd better walk him since he hadn't been out for a dozen hours or so. He was in full agreement, finished before we got halfway to Mrs. Garabaldi's, and we made it back into the apartment before my landlady-turned-literary-critic could assail me with more observations about the mail.

I got in the car and drove to the Ohio River, then crossed over it on the Clay Wade Bailey Bridge, which is just half a mile past the I-71/I-75 bridge and a hell of a lot less crowded. When you're halfway across either bridge you're suddenly in Kentucky, but the river towns of Covington and Newport are really just extensions of Cincinnati's downtown, with some excellent advantages. Kentucky's where I always went to buy my liquor and cigarettes, and gas was usually a few cents cheaper too.

I got off the bridge, turned onto Third Street, and made my way to Delahunt's office. It was a self-contained building that could have used a little cleaning and updating, but that made it fit in with the rest of the neighborhood. I parked on the street about a block from the office, put a quarter in the meter—Jim Simmons couldn't fix my tickets on this side of the river—walked past a long row of parked cars, came to the office, and entered.

A middle-aged receptionist greeted me without getting up from her desk.

"Good morning, sir, and welcome to Delahunt Realty. How may we help you?"

"I'd like to see Mr. Delahunt," I said.

"I'm afraid he's not here," she replied. "Perhaps our Mr. Benson can help you?"

Before I could stop her she'd pushed a button on her desk, and a moment later Mr. Benson, a blond six-footer, appeared in the doorway behind her.

"May I help you, Mr. . . . . ?" he said pleasantly.

"I don't want to cause any bother," I said. "I was here the other day." I turned to the receptionist. "You were at lunch, or at least out of the office."

"And who did you see, sir?" asked Benson.

"Mr. Delahunt," I said, and they exchanged looks. "I'm afraid I left my pen in his office. It's not worth much, but it was my father's and it has a sentimental value to me. I wonder if I might look for it? I'll just be a minute."

"All right, whoever the hell you are!" snapped Benson. "What the hell do you want?"

"I just told you," I said.

"Abner Delahunt hasn't been here in over a week, so you weren't talking to him the other day. If you're another creditor, either get the hell out, or we can call the cops and let them sort it out."

"All right, all right," I said. "You saw through me. But you tell that bastard I'll be seeing him in court!"

I turned and left before they could say anything else.

Well, I thought as I walked down the street to my car, maybe he had a gun hidden in his office and maybe he didn't. Probably Sorrentino and I would have to do a little reconnoitering at two or three in the morning, and if we saw it, leave it where it was and have Simmons tell the Covington cops to look for it.

As I was walking back to the car a jewelry store on the other side of the street caught my eye. Well, actually what caught it was the very tasteful display in the window. I knew just enough about jewelry stores to know that when you had the goods, you didn't need garish displays. So I crossed the street and stared into the window. Diamonds, rubies, pearls, rings, and necklaces, all sedately displayed. The sign said "Mela Jewelers—Orestes Mela, Proprietor." I entered and saw a balding man in a vest waiting on a couple. I browsed for about five minutes until they'd made their purchase and left.

"Can I help you?" he asked.

"I certainly hope so," I said. "I'm looking for some diamonds."

"*Some?*" he asked.

I nodded. "About a million dollars' worth," I answered. "They were attached to a cat's collar. You know anything about them?"

He looked like I'd just shot his best friend.

"I knew someone would come looking for them sooner or later." He sighed deeply. What took you so long?"

23.

"Lock up the store," I said. "We need to talk."

He walked out from behind the counter, crossed over to the door, hung up an "Out to Lunch" sign, and locked the door.

"Are you Covington or Newport police?" he asked.

"Other side of the river," I said.

He nodded. "Yes, he lives there, doesn't he?"

"For the moment," I said. "I think the police will supply him with somewhat less luxurious living quarters."

He frowned. "You say that as if you're not one of them."

I pulled out my license. "I'm working for the owner of the diamonds."

"Ah," he said, nodding again.

"You want to tell me about it?"

"Yes, I suppose I'd better," said Mela.

"Yes, I suppose you had."

"I've known Mr. Delahunt for a few years. He bought his wife a lovely bracelet from me about, oh, three years ago. And twice since then he's bought other unique items, but I don't think they were for Mrs. Delahunt."

"Probably not," I agreed.

"Then last week he brought me the oddest thing," said Mela.

"A cat's collar?"

He nodded. "Studded with diamonds. Not rhinestones, not cheap imitations, but the real thing."

"How many?" I asked, though I knew the answer.

"Ten," he replied. "He asked me to take them off, so I did. He also

167

asked me to use one in a ring." He paused and lowered his voice, though we were the only two people in the store. "I think it was for his latest girlfriend."

"It was," I said. "I've seen it. Very nice work."

"Thank you."

"Let me ask you a question, Mr. Mela," I said. "Did he show you proof of ownership, anything to suggest the diamonds were his?"

He suddenly looked very nervous. "No," he said, shaking his head. "I suspect that's why you're here." He looked intently at me. "How much trouble is Mr. Delahunt in?" And then, "How much trouble am *I* in?"

"You're not in any trouble at all if you cooperate," I said and hoped I was telling the truth.

He pulled out a handkerchief and wiped some sweat from his face. "*That's* a relief. I have certainly never knowingly broken any laws."

"I realize your answer will just be an estimate," I continued, "but based on your experience and expertise, how much would you say the diamonds were worth?"

He considered it for a moment. "Perhaps eighty-five to ninety thousand apiece. In a bull market, which we haven't had since before Bush's last year, perhaps a hundred thousand."

"There's no way they could possibly be worth more?"

"How much more?"

"A million apiece?"

He chuckled dryly. "Is that what Abner Delahunt told you?"

"I've never met the man," I answered. "That's what the original owner said they were worth."

"He was lying or deluded," said Mela.

"You've worked on a lot of million-dollar diamonds?" I asked.

He shook his head. "No. Hell, I'd be afraid to *work* on them, as you say. But I've seen some and have actually appraised a pair for a family in Indian Hill."

"They came all the way to Covington for an appraisal?"

He drew himself up to his full height. "I *am* Orestes Mela," he said with all the dignity he could muster, which was considerable.

"No insult intended," I assured him.

"None taken," he lied graciously.

"So you took all ten diamonds off the collar," I said. "One you made into a ring."

"That's not quite accurate. I had the ring in stock. I took out a faux stone the size of the diamond and replaced it."

"Okay," I said. "That accounts for one of the diamonds. What about the other nine?"

"Mr. Delahunt went out for lunch while I put the diamond in the ring and removed the rest. When he came back he asked me if I wanted to buy any of them. I said I couldn't begin to pay market value and make a profit, but that I would take three of them for fifty thousand apiece, and he agreed on the spot. The other six I gave to him when he left with the ring."

"And you still have the three you bought?" I asked.

He nodded. "Yes."

"I'm afraid the police are going to confiscate them," I said.

"I know," he replied unhappily.

"And I very much doubt that Delahunt will be able to return your hundred and fifty thousand."

"I gave him thirty thousand down and was to pay him thirty a month for the next four months."

"So you're not as bad off as you might be."

"I made the transaction without proof of ownership. He swore he'd bring it in the next time he was at his office across the street. I've been there twice since then, but he hasn't returned." He looked at me, and I could see that he was actually shaking. "I don't want to go to jail, Mr. Paxton. Believe me, I acted in good faith."

"That's not up to me to decide," I said. "Hell, I don't even know what the law is. But I'll be happy to testify that you were open and aboveboard, that you hid nothing, and that you acted in good faith. I think going to his office will speak to your integrity, and the fact that you can turn over the three diamonds will certainly be in your favor."

"Thank goodness!" he said, going a little weak in the knees and supporting himself on the counter. "You can't know how worried I've been the past few days when he didn't show up and I was unable to contact him. If I went to the police and he was either ill or legitimately detained . . ." He shook his head. "And if he truly didn't have the papers, am I an accomplice?"

I laid a steadying hand on his shoulder. "It'll be all right, Mr. Mela," I said. Suddenly I smiled. "And I thought all jewelers had to worry about was getting robbed."

He chuckled at that. "You wouldn't believe all the things we worry about."

"I'm starting to get an idea," I said.

There was a brief silence.

"What now?" he asked.

"May I see the diamonds? I'd just like to see what three hundred thousand dollars' worth of diamonds looks like."

"Closer to a quarter million," he said. "Come with me."

We went into a back room, a very tidy office, where he kept a state-of-the-art safe. I looked away while he opened it and pulled out a little black velvet tray with three diamonds that looked just like the one Mitzi Cramer had on her finger.

"Impressive," I said.

"And they were all on a cat's collar," he said, shaking his head in wonderment. "What if the cat had run off?"

"I gather she was never outside," I answered. *Until the night of the murder.*

He reached into the safe and pulled something else out.

"Here," he said. "You might as well have this. Or throw it out if you prefer."

"What is it?" I asked as he held up a little leather strap.

"The collar," he said. He indicated a shiny little tag. "It's still got the license on."

He handed it to me, I glanced at it briefly and stuck it in a pocket, he put the diamonds back in the safe and locked it.

"Now what?" he asked as we left the office and returned to the shop.

"Now I tell the cops I'm working with," I said. "They're on the Cincinnati side of the river, and the diamonds were stolen from a Cincinnati house. They'll have to work it out with the Covington police to see who has jurisdiction over this part of the case."

"This part of the case?" he repeated.

"It's about more than the diamonds," I said, and told him about the murder. He looked even more nervous, if possible. "Anyway, somebody will be by in the next day or two to take your statement and pick up the goods."

"The goods?" he repeated with a grimace. "That makes them sound so common. Maybe they're not worth a million apiece, or even quite a hundred thousand, but they are damned fine stones."

"Please tell the diamonds that I meant no insult," I said.

He laughed at that, then shook my hand. "You've taken a huge load off my mind, Mr. Paxton."

"That's what us Humphrey Bogart types do," I replied with a smile.

And we also, I decided, *put in for the finder's fee before our less fussy partner can walk in, shoot the place up, and run off with the diamonds and anything else that catches his eye.*

Marlowe wasn't there, of course, but in retrospect I knew exactly what his expression would have been.

24.

I had a totally noncommittal lunch with Sorrentino. I mentioned that I'd tried Delahunt's office across the river with no success.

"I didn't even know he *had* an office in Kentucky," said Sorrentino.

"Neither did I until this morning," I said. "How about you? Got anything at all?"

He shook his head. "Not a thing. Those diamonds could be in Peru or Pakistan for all I know. I never saw anything that valuable vanish that fast. You'd think ten million worth couldn't stay hidden that long, that *some*one would say something."

"From everything we've been able to find out about them, they're worth a million, tops," I said. "You know that."

"I know, I know," he said with a weary sigh. "But damn it, Eli, he *said* ten mil, and he sure as hell didn't sound like he was lying."

"I've seen one of the diamonds," I said. "We've both seen the insurance form."

"I don't buy it," he said.

"Why the hell not?" I shot back. "We *know* the one that Mitzi Cramer's got is worth a hundred grand, tops."

"I know what it's worth, and I know what the insurance papers say, but there's one thing we haven't really considered," said Sorrentino. "Why did the Bolivian drug cartel send expensive hitters after a million? They'd figure one man could handle it. But," he added, leaning forward, "if it's ten million, three hitters ensures that one of them won't be running off with the loot."

"And that's all you've got to go on?" I asked.

"That, and the fact that Palanto had no reason to lie to me."

"Maybe he was afraid you might shoot him and run off with the cat," I said. "After all, someone did."

"I could do it just as easily for one mil," said Sorrentino. "And I just can't buy that the Bolivians would send three hitters over for just a million."

"Hell, maybe they're the kind of guys who'd have sent three men over for fifty grand, the kind who don't let anyone rip them off even for lunch money," I said. "We both know there are certain New York families that would feel that way."

"Maybe." He looked unconvinced, and finally shrugged. "What the hell. First we've got to find them. Then we'll worry about what they're worth." He paused. "What about dinner?"

"What have you got a taste for?" I asked.

"Diamonds."

"What else?"

He smiled. "Italian, I think."

"Okay, there are a couple of Carrabba's in town," I said. "I'm sure you've got 'em in Chicago."

"Yeah, that'll be fine."

I told him how to get to the closest one, and we agreed to meet at six, since there was an NBA double-header starting at 7:30 on ESPN. He picked up the tab, as usual, and we left.

I waited until he had pulled out, then got into my car and drove right to the station. A minute later I was sitting across from Jim Simmons, waiting for him to get off the phone.

"Well, two-thirds of our Bolivian problem has been taken care of," he told me when he hung up the receiver.

"How?" I asked.

"The Feds made a deal," he replied.

"The Feds?"

"State, I suppose. I don't know. They don't talk much to little folks, like cops who put their lives on the line every day." He took a sip from a can of Diet Pepsi he had on his desk. "Anyway, the deal was we'd put them on a plane for home this afternoon if they didn't fight deportation."

"As simple as that?" I said. "It's missing some details."

"We agreed not to prosecute—they had no permits for their guns, and they were wanted by Interpol—and the feds agreed to keep the whole incident quiet. I get the feeling they're going right from our calaboose to one in La Paz."

"And if their cartel has half the strength of the bigger Mexican and Colombian ones, they'll be out an hour later."

"Not our problem," said Simmons. "But if I were them, I'd be happier in jail than explaining to my bosses how I managed to get identified and arrested in a foreign country—especially before I got what I'd been sent there for."

"Speaking of that," I said, "I know where they are."

He frowned. "The Bolivians? I just told you."

"The diamonds," I said.

"Diamonds?" he repeated, frowning. "What diamonds?"

"I'll come to them," I said. I paused and gave him a great big grin. "And I know who killed Big Jim Palanto."

"Palanto?" he repeated. "You mean Pepperidge."

I smiled. "No, *you* mean Palanto."

"Okay, Palanto," he said. "Now suppose you tell me what you think you know?"

"He was killed by a neighbor," I said.

"The guy you had Bill Calhoun hunting up for you?"

I nodded. "A realtor named Abner Delahunt."

"Okay," said Simmons. "What did they fight over?"

"I doubt that they fought over anything," I said. "I think Delahunt knew that Velma—Mrs. Pepperidge—was out at her bridge club the night of the blizzard, walked the hundred yards or so from his house to Palanto's, rang the bell, and was invited in, which is why there was no sign of breaking and entering. They were, if not friends, at least acquaintances, belonged to the same golf club, the same church, probably the same businessmen's clubs. He had to have been there before, because he knew exactly what he was after."

"You got any proof for anything you've said so far, Eli?" asked Simmons dubiously.

I grinned at him. "I got a proposition for you, Jim."

"Oh?"

"Yeah," I said. "The Bengals close out their season at home in a couple of weeks against the Browns. If I don't hand you the killer all wrapped up nice and neat, I'll pop for two tickets."

"And I pay if you give me the murderer?"

I nodded. "Right."

He reached across the desk. "You got yourself a deal, Eli—and I hope it's my treat."

"It will be," I assured him.

"Okay, go on."

"I don't know how Delahunt got Palanto out on that balcony. Probably, given that Palanto was an amateur stargazer, he simply didn't stop him. The house was empty, so I don't suppose it made any difference to Delahunt where he killed him."

"So Palanto goes out to look at the stars, or the storm, or whatever the hell he looked at through his telescope, and Delahunt drilled him, two shots right through the heart," continued Simmons. He took another sip of his Pepsi. "It *sounds* good, Eli, but so far I haven't heard anything like, for example, proof."

"I'm coming to it," I told him. "Anyway, that was the situation when I got there after you called me in the middle of the night: Palanto dead in the snow, and no trace of the killer."

"Right. Now what can you add to that?"

"There was also no trace of the cat. Remember? That's why you called me. Because Velma was desperate for it . . . until I found it and returned it to her." I paused again. "That's when she had me arrested."

"I remember."

"But you don't know *why*."

"Enlighten me," said Simmons.

"That cat had a million dollars' worth of diamonds on its collar."

"You're kidding!" he exclaimed.

"No, Jim, I'm not. And Delahunt not only knew that, but he was desperate for cash. His business was going down the tubes, he was in a race to sell his house before it was repossessed, and he owed money all over town."

"Go on."

"Right after the murder, he gives his girlfriend a ring with a diamond that's valued near a hundred grand."

"Have you seen it?" he asked.

I nodded. "It, and *her*. She makes Bettie Page look like a boy."

"Is she in town?"

"Yeah," I said. "Her name's Mitzi Cramer." He scribbled down her name, then did the same when I gave him her address.

"Okay," he said. "That's one diamond. Maybe it's from the collar, maybe it's not."

"Oh, it is," I assured him.

"How do you know?"

"I got the insurance papers from Velma, and according to a jeweler named Winslow Monroe it's a perfect match."

"How does he know?"

"She tried to sell it to him."

"Less than a week after she got it?" he said dubiously.

"The girl's loyalty knows no bounds," I said. "Of course, neither does Delahunt's. He's a married man—for a few more weeks or months, anyway."

"It all sounds logical, Eli," said Simmons, "but you'd better have more than this. One diamond may or may not be from the cat's collar, and a girl who's maybe sleeping with Delahunt is wearing it on her finger. That's a little *too* circumstantial."

"Oh?"

"What about the other nine diamonds?"

"I found the jeweler who took 'em off the collar for Delahunt," I said. "He's got three of them, and he'll testify he set a fourth in Mitzi Cramer's ring."

Simmons's eyes widened. "No bullshit?" he said. "He'll testify to that?"

"Right."

"What about the other six diamonds?"

"Delahunt took them after the jeweler—his name's Orestes Mela—took 'em off." I gave him my biggest Sunday-go-to-church grin. "I'd like something on the fifty-yard line, I think."

"Jesus, Eli!" he said. "I don't know how the hell you did it, but if the Cramer girl and especially this Mela can corroborate what you said, you've not only got your tickets, but I'll treat you to the best steak at the Precinct after the game."

"Always assuming the Bengals win," I said. "Otherwise we'll be too depressed to eat."

"If everything you've told me holds up, I'll make sure you make the front page of the *Cincinnati Enquirer* two or three days running. *That* ought to get a little traffic to your office."

"Jesus!" I said suddenly.

"What is it?" he asked.

"I've spent so much time on this thing, I haven't been to my office in a week." Then I shrugged. "What the hell. It's six, two and even that no one else has been there either."

He chuckled. "So where do we find this Orestes Mela?"

"He's in Covington," I said.

"Shit!" he muttered. "That'll take a couple of extra days of paperwork."

"What if I bring him here tomorrow?" I said. "Voluntarily?"

"It'd make things go a lot faster," he said. "We'll still have to do the paperwork, but if we can get his statement on record we can arrest Delahunt before he can fly the coop."

"I'll get him here first thing in the morning," I said.

He shook his head. "No, I've got a departmental meeting, something about a couple of teen gangs not that far from your neighborhood. By the way, do you think Delahunt is in any danger?"

"The remaining Bolivian doesn't know about him, and neither does my friend Sorrentino. If his wife doesn't pull out a driver and pretend his head is a golf ball, he's probably safe for the time being."

He considered my answer, then nodded his head. "Okay, we'll give him a little more rope. How's two o'clock tomorrow?"

"Two o'clock tomorrow?" I said. "It's a date."

"Okay," he said, getting up and starting to walk me to his office door.

"One more thing," I said.

"What?"

"I've kept my friend from Chicago in the dark about Mela," I said. "Theoretically, we're splitting the finder's fee from the insurance company."

He frowned. "You're cutting him out?" he asked. "That's not like you, Eli."

I shook my head. "No, I'm not cutting him out. But I think there's at least a possibility that if he sees the diamonds before I deliver them here, he may decide that one hundred percent is better than ten percent, if you see what I mean."

"Okay, I see what you mean."

"So you don't talk to the press, or even anyone else on the force, until I deliver Mela and the remaining diamonds to you tomorrow afternoon."

He shook my hand again. "It's a deal."

I went home, let Mrs. Cominsky tell me how the mail was finally losing its shock value, and took Marlowe for a walk. When we got done we went back up to the apartment, I took his leash off and wrapped it around the front doorknob as usual, walked into the kitchen, and popped open a beer for me. Mrs. Cominsky had forced a bottle of eggnog on me the day before to prove that even letter-writing perverts couldn't rob her of the Christmas spirit, so I opened it and poured about a pint into a soup bowl for Marlowe.

"And tomorrow," I told him as he lapped up the eggnog in record time, "all I have to do is deliver a jeweler who wants to talk to a cop who wants to listen, and when that's done, I'll buy you a rib eye of your very own."

He gave me a look that said, *Dreamer* and went back to sleep.

I should have paid attention to him.

25.

I met Sorrentino for lunch at an O'Charley's. We talked football and basketball all the way through the meal and started in on horse racing just as we were finishing our desserts.

"Not a bad meal," he said, wiping his mouth off and crushing his napkin into a shapeless ball.

"You should try this place on the weekend," I said. "That's when they serve their prime rib." I paused. "Except . . ."

"Except?"

"Except you may be on your way home before then."

"I'm not throwing in the towel yet," he said, taking a swallow of his beer.

"I know."

Suddenly he leaned forward. "You found something out?"

I nodded.

"Okay, spill it!"

"You know the police headquarters building?" I said.

"Yeah."

"Be there at two o'clock this afternoon. Ask for Jim Simmons's office. I'll meet you there."

"What have you got?" he demanded.

"I'll lay it all out for you there," I said. "No sense doing it twice, once for you and once for Jim."

"Why meet me?" he said. "Why don't we just go together?"

"I have something I've got to do," I said. "Don't worry. I'll be there, and hopefully I'll have this all cleared up by then." *And you're not going to stop me from giving the diamonds to Jim in his own office, no matter how much you'd like to keep them.*

"All right," he said at last. "If I have to wait an hour, I have to wait an hour." He laid some cash on the bill and got to his feet. "Don't be late."

"I'll be there," I assured him.

He left. I made a quick pit stop in the men's room, then went out to my car, started it up, promised it that it'd have that new transmission any day now, and headed south to the Clay Bailey Bridge. Seven minutes later I'd parked a few doors down from Mela's, got out, and walked to the store.

It occurred to me that I hadn't seen any assistants, I hadn't checked his hours, and for all I knew he took a three-hour lunch, but there was a small, tasteful "Open" sign on the door, and I walked in.

"Mr. Paxton," he said. "I've been expecting you."

"Call me Eli," I replied.

"All right, Eli," he said. "And I am Orestes."

"You want to close the shop, Orestes?" I suggested.

He nodded his agreement, walked over and locked the door, then took down the "Open" sign and replaced it with a "Closed" one.

"Come on to the back," he said, heading to his office. I followed him, then sat on a chair while he opened his safe and pulled out the velvet box with the three diamonds. "I hope he's not so broke that I can't get my thirty thousand dollars back," he remarked. "But even if he is, I'm almost glad to be rid of them. I've had a very uneasy feeling since I made the down payment that no good could possibly come of this." Suddenly a frown—a very frightened frown—crossed his face. "I'm not criminally culpable, am I?"

"No," I said. "He told you in good faith that he'd supply proof of ownership, you didn't try to sell them, and you agreed to cooperate with the police the moment I approached you. I don't think you're in any legal danger at all. All the cops want is for you to tell them exactly what you told me yesterday and maybe repeat it in court if Delahunt is dumb enough to plead innocent."

"Oh, I will," he assured me. "My wife has been urging me to go to the police even before you showed up yesterday." He paused. "I am an honest man, Mr. Paxton."

"Eli," I corrected him. "And I'm sure you're an honest man. You're just working in an industry that occasionally attracts dishonest men."

"I'm sure you deal with them every day," said Mela.

"I'm sure we all do," I answered. "The trick is spotting them."

"You know," said Mela, "I've been selling the occasional piece to Mr. Delahunt for years. He always paid on the spot, he had a fine reputation, offices all over Cincinnati as well as the big one right across the street here, a lovely wife. What makes a man like that become a criminal?"

"A fine reputation is no substitute for a fine mind when the economy goes south," I answered. "As for his lovely wife, if he drops dead tomorrow she'll be the first to dance on his grave."

He shook his head. "I don't understand it. I've been married to my Teresa for thirty-one years, and in my eyes she grows more beautiful every day. Why do so many men my age turn their backs on their wives and have tawdry affairs with young women?"

"They get the women's youth and beauty, at least temporarily," I answered. "And one way or another the women get a piece of their fortune, usually permanently."

"And what do the wives get?"

"A good lawyer, if they're smart," I said.

He sighed deeply. "I suppose so, though that's a very cynical answer. But it's not fair."

"You think it's not fair *now*, you should have seen it before there were community property laws and pre-nup contracts," I said with a smile.

"Surely you don't have one with your wife," said Mela.

"I didn't have one even when I was married," I answered.

"You're divorced?" he said. "I didn't . . . I meant no insult."

"Different situation," I said. "She left *before* I had any money." I felt a rueful smile cross my face. "Hell, I still don't have any."

"What will happen to Mr. Delahunt?" he asked suddenly.

I shrugged. "If he cops a plea and behaves himself in jail, I suppose he could be out in fifteen years or so, if he lives that long. If he fights it and it goes to trial and he's found guilty, it's up to the jury. A case like this, given that the victim had ties with organized crime, I would think the death penalty's out of the question, but I could see him getting life, with or without parole if it's first degree—and given the circumstances, it's pretty hard to see the prosecution agreeing on second-degree or manslaughter."

"You really think so?" he asked.

I nodded and patted the velvet box where it lay on the table. "This'll do the trick. Before yesterday, we didn't even have him on a cat-napping charge."

"It's hard to believe that he actually had all these diamonds strapped around a cat's neck."

"Yeah," I agreed. "I just wish he had nine more like it."

"I beg your pardon?" he said.

"Private joke."

"Well," said Mela, "I suppose we should be going."

I checked my watch. It was one-thirty.

"Yeah," I said. "We'll be about fifteen minutes early, but it beats the hell out of being late. He knows I'm bringing you and the diamonds in. If 2:05 rolls around and I'm not there, he'll be sending out search parties."

"So we have fifteen minutes?" he said.

"Right."

"Then let me waste five of them," he said, walking back to the safe and opening it. A few seconds later he pulled out a bottle and a couple of gorgeous crystal goblets.

"Napoleon brandy," he said, filling the two goblets. "To celebrate the end of this incident."

I picked up my goblet and sniffed the brandy. It smelled like any other brandy, but I'm no connoisseur. "To your very good health, Orestes," I said, holding it up.

"And to yours, Eli," he replied, and we clicked the goblets together and each took a swallow.

"Well?" he said, looking at me anxiously. "What do you think of it?"

"It went down smooth as silk," I said. "I could make a habit of this stuff."

"I save it for special occasions," he said. "Knowing that I'm on the same side as the police qualifies as special, given some of the fears I've been living with for the past week."

We drained the goblets, and I checked my watch again.

"Twenty to," I said. "We'd better go."

He nodded his agreement, put the goblets in a small sink, shut and locked the safe, and led the way to the front door.

As we walked out to the sidewalk, a shot rang out. Mela screamed, grabbed his shoulder, and slammed back into the door, sliding down to the ground.

"Hit the dirt, Eli!" yelled Sorrentino as half a dozen more shots whizzed by.

26.

I dove to the sidewalk just as I heard an agonized scream off to my left. I turned my head just in time to see a geyser of blood spurting out of "Mr. Smith's" neck.

"Damn!" grunted Sorrentino. I looked in the other direction and saw Sorrentino clutching his chest as blood seeped out through his fingers.

I got up and surveyed the carnage around me. The Bolivian was lying stock-still, covered with blood, but it wasn't gushing anymore. Mela was on his knees, and I could see he'd been shot in the arm. I checked; it was the fleshy part. It would hurt like hell, but there was nothing broken.

"I'll be right back," I told him, and raced over to Sorrentino as I heard the sound of approaching sirens.

"There'll be an ambulance here in a minute," I told him. "Just hang on."

"The Bolivian?" he grated.

"Dead."

"Good," he said, and lost consciousness.

I went back to Mela. "You okay?" I asked.

"Really just a scratch," he said. "I fell down from surprise, not pain. I'll be all right." He looked at Sorrentino and the Bolivian sprawled out, blood-soaked, and motionless on the ground. "Are there any more of them, or is that it?"

"That's it," I assured him as a cop car pulled up.

Two cops got out of the car, guns in hands. "You!" he yelled at me. "Facedown on the ground, hands behind your head!"

I did as he ordered. He turned to his partner. "Call an ambulance."

Then he reconsidered. "Make it two. And some backup." He leaned over me and snapped a pair of cuffs around my wrists. "What the hell's going on here?"

"I'm a private investigator," I said. "My license is in my wallet, and you can check on me with Jim Simmons or Bill Calhoun in Cincinnati Police Headquarters. I'm working on a case." I nodded my head toward the Bolivian. "That one is a killer. This one—" I indicated Sorrentino "—saved us and needs medical attention pretty damned quick. And this man—" I nodded toward Mela "—is Orestes Mela, the owner of this jewelry shop. He's who the killer was after, and he's going to need medical attention too."

The other cop examined the Bolivian. "This one's dead."

An ambulance pulled up and quickly placed Sorrentino onto a stretcher, attached him to an IV and oxygen, and loaded him into the vehicle. The backup police car arrived as they were doing it.

"This guy's in a bad way," said one of the medics. He turned to Mela. "You can wait. There's another ambulance on the way, but we've got to get this man into surgery quick."

Mela nodded. "Go. I'll be all right."

The ambulance was racing off ten seconds later, and as it turned the corner another one pulled up, checked with the cops, helped Mela into the back, and drove away.

"Where are they going?" I asked.

"St. Elizabeth," answered a cop. "They're closest, and they've got a trauma center."

"It's damned uncomfortable, lying on my stomach. Can I get up now?"

"Yeah," said the cop, helping me to my feet. "Slowly and carefully."

"Thanks," I muttered.

"Okay," said the cop. "We'll wait for someone to scoop up the body and take it to the morgue, and then we're going to have a long talk down at the station."

"Can I make a suggestion?" I said.

"What?" he asked suspiciously.

"Have Lieutenant Jim Simmons of the Cincinnati police notified about what happened here. He's waiting in his office for me to bring the jeweler in."

"The jeweler?" he repeated. "He's behind all this?"

I shook my head. "No . . . but he's got information on a murder that took place a week ago on the other side of the river."

"And this guy's the killer?" he asked, nudging the corpse with his toe.

"No. He's a hitter, but he didn't commit the murder in Cincinnati."

He peered at the Bolivian. "Looks like just another Mexican enforcer. We're getting our share of them these days. Maybe we ought to legalize drugs, the way they did out in . . . I don't know, Utah, was it?"

"Colorado," I told him. "And this guy's not Mexican."

He peered at the corpse. "Oh?"

"Bolivian. And definitely a killer."

"If he wasn't before, he will be by tomorrow," said the cop. "I don't think your friend will make it to midnight."

A truck pulled up and carted the corpse off to the morgue, and then the cops drove me to the local station.

"What the hell was this all about?" asked the second cop when we were all seated in an interrogation room.

"It's complicated," I said.

"We've got time."

"Okay," I said. "There's a murder investigation going on across the river. Turns out that Mr. Mela was sitting on the motive. I was just taking him to police headquarters to turn over the evidence and make a statement, which ought to be enough to bring our man to court."

"The evidence?"

"Three diamonds," I said, since the hospital was going to find them anyway. "They're in a black velvet box in his coat pocket."

I stopped speaking, and after maybe twenty seconds one of the cops said, "What else?"

"It gets really complex," I said. "Our suspect killed a former mafioso and stole some diamonds. What he didn't know was that the mafioso had stolen them, or their equivalent, from a Bolivian drug cartel, which sent three hitters here to get them back. Two of the hitters have been deported. The dead man was the third."

"Hard to imagine that Mela would handle hot diamonds," said another cop. "He's got a helluva reputation as a decent, honest man."

"He deserves the reputation," I said. "He didn't know they were hot. That's why he was coming with me—to hand the diamonds over and make a statement."

They queried me for another hour and a half, going over the details again and again, looking for anything that didn't jibe, that didn't agree with what I'd said before. Finally, another cop came into the room.

"Okay," he announced. "I've spoken to Lieutenant Simmons, and he confirms as much of your story as he *can* confirm."

"Thanks for believing me," I said as I got to my feet.

He smiled. "Officially we're just giving you enough rope to hang yourself," he said. "But unofficially, I recognized your name from your license. I read about you and how you solved that Trojan colt thing the last time you paid our state a visit." He reached out and shook my hand. "I hope you get your man."

I signed a few more forms. Then one of the cops drove me back to my car and told me the quickest way to get to St. Elizabeth's. I probably broke a couple of speed laws getting there, pulled into the lot, then entered the building and asked for Sorrentino at the desk.

"I'm sorry," said the receptionist. "We don't have a Valentine Sorrentino here."

"He was just admitted into the emergency room a couple of hours ago," I said.

"Oh," she said, pulling up some other list on her computer. Suddenly she frowned. "Yes, we have Mr. Sorrentino here. He's in intensive care."

"So he's alive!" I said. "That's a relief. How do I get to intensive care from here?"

"His condition is grave," she said, still looking at the screen. "I'm afraid he's not allowed any visitors."

"Fuck that!" I snapped. "He's my friend, and I want to see him!"

"Don't use such language on me!" she snapped back. "And you can't see him."

I flashed my trusty detective's license. "I *have* to speak to him," I said. "And if I have to arrest you for obstructing justice, I'm prepared to do so, and I hope you've got a good lawyer."

And like a hundred others who saw the license and couldn't tell the difference between detective and cop, she gave in, had her machine print up some kind of pass that would let me in to Sorrentino's room, and got an attendant to lead me there.

I opened the door and walked in. Sorrentino was lying there, his eyes shut, bandages all the hell over his chest, a bunch of tubes running into him, with one going up his nose. A young blonde nurse was reading the dials or screens or whatever on some machine he was hooked up to.

"I've got to talk to him," I told her.

She looked at the pass and nodded her assent. "Three minutes," she said, walking to the door. "No more."

Then she was out in the corridor, closing the door behind her, and I was alone with Sorrentino.

"How did the surgery go?" I asked.

He almost grinned. "How the hell do I know?" he half-whispered. "I slept through the whole thing."

"I'm sorry, Val."

This time he *did* smile. "*You're* sorry?"

"You saved my life," I said. "But what the hell were you doing there?"

"When you didn't agree to go to Simmons right from lunch, I figured you'd found the diamonds, so I drove around the block when we left the restaurant and followed you. You never saw me." He coughed weakly. "Damned lucky I did follow you. The Bolivian must have been tracking you too."

"I'm sorry I kept you in the dark about it," I said.

He gasped for air. "Probably thought I'd grab the diamonds and take 'em back to Chicago instead of claiming the finder's fee?"

I nodded. "Yes, I did."

"Did he have the other nine?"

"No, just three of them."

"Can't trust nobody these days." He coughed again, even more weakly this time. "Including me. I *had* planned to take the diamonds back to Chicago." He paused, wincing in pain. "On the other hand, if I'd played it fair and square, you'd be dead now."

"I know."

"And because of that, I have a last request."

"Screw the last requests," I said. "You'll be up and around in two weeks."

"Don't bullshit me, Eli," he said. "We both know I'll be dead before morning."

"Okay," I said, suddenly aware of the sound of machinery whirring, machinery that was keeping him temporarily alive. "No more bullshit. What can I do for you?"

"I've got two daughters," he said. "I haven't seen them since my wife left me four years ago, and I haven't been as good about sending them money as I should have been. This is my chance—my last chance—to make amends." He made an effort to open his eyes, which kept falling shut. "I know it's only three diamonds instead of nine, but that's three more than we had yesterday." A tear—of pain, of regret, who knows?—trickled down his cheek. "Give them the finder's fee."

"I will, Val."

"Shake on it, partner," he said.

I reached over and took his hand in mine. It went totally limp while I was shaking it, the machine whirred and transmitted a Code Blue to the staff. I heard footsteps racing toward the door, and I knew that my friend was dead.

27.

I stopped by Orestes Mela's room. His wound was little more than a scratch, but the hospital was keeping him overnight just to be on the safe side. He seemed in reasonably good spirits for a peaceful, law-abiding guy who'd just been shot by either a Bolivian hit man or a Chicago mafioso. (The bullet had just grazed his arm—the part we call the bicep on boxers and body builders—and was probably lodged in the store's exterior wall if the CSI guys hadn't dug it out yet. I supposed it didn't make much difference whose bullet it was at this late date, since both shooters were dead.)

"I'd give you the diamonds," he said apologetically, "but they took everything I had in my pockets—my wallet, my comb, even my jeweler's eyepiece, when they put me in this gown in the emergency room, and of course they took the box with the diamonds too. I'll be able to pick them up when I'm released tomorrow morning."

"The local cops know about the diamonds and have probably confiscated them by now," I told him. "The Cincinnati police will do the paperwork and get the diamonds in a week or two, and there's no way Delahunt goes to trial in less than a few months, so that can't hurt the case. Are you still willing to come to Cincinnati police headquarters with me when you get out of here and make your statement?" I half-expected that being shot would have soured him on the whole thing.

"Absolutely!" he said firmly. "If it wasn't for Abner Delahunt, I wouldn't be sitting here with my arm in a sling—and feeling incredibly lucky that it's nothing worse. Check with my doctor or nurse or whoever you have to check with, find out what time they're releasing me tomorrow, and be waiting for me in the lobby."

"You got it," I said, walking to the door. "You're a good man, Orestes."

"I don't know how good I am," he said. "But I am by God an honest one."

I saluted him, which seemed to please him enormously. Then I checked with a nurse who was passing by, waited a minute while she hunted down whoever it was that actually knew when Mela would be allowed to leave, and told me that it would be ten in the morning. I thanked her and went out to my car.

I was feeling pretty down. I'd lost a friend, one who'd risked and lost his life to save mine. And because I owed him my life, I knew I'd keep my word to him, and that meant there'd be no finder's fee for me. Except for Velma's retainer, I'd been working for free for a week.

There was no sense going to headquarters, not without Mela and the diamonds. I stopped at the Twenty Yard Line, ordered a beer, and borrowed the bar's phone long enough to call Jim Simmons and tell him what had happened and that I'd be by with Mela but without the diamonds at about ten-thirty in the morning. He knew about the shootings, asked a bunch of questions, expressed some almost-sincere sympathy at the loss of Sorrentino even though he was a monster, and told me he'd be waiting for us in the morning.

I finished the beer, went back to the car, and tried to think. Was there anything else I had to do on this idiot, nonprofit case?

And I realized there was one last thing, even though I wasn't the least bit interested in doing it. But Velma had paid me fifteen hundred dollars, and as much as I didn't like her, I figured I owed it to her to tell her about the diamonds. And the fact that I could all but guarantee that she'd never see at least six of them again was my reward for facing her one more time.

I figured I'd been gone too long, and I'd better stop by the apartment and walk Marlowe first. Mrs. Garabaldi actually blew us a kiss when he drenched her petunias, and I almost made it back up the stairs before Mrs. Cominsky could complain about today's batch of perverts while refusing to turn the letters over to the vice squad, or to me, or to anyone except perhaps Mrs. Garabaldi.

I finally made it into the apartment, saw that Marlowe's food bowl was empty, opened a can of pork and beans and poured it in. I remembered that I hadn't shaved in three days and stopped by the bathroom long enough to take some of the fuzz off, turned on the TV to see if we were at war with anyone, and finally ran out of reasons and excuses not to drive over to the Pepperidge house.

It was dark when I got there. I pulled up the driveway, got out, and went to the front door. It had the kind of knocker on it that you'd swear was made to be looked at rather than used, and I rang the bell. About thirty seconds later the door opened, and I found myself facing Velma's very formidable figure and thinking the bullet that grazed Mela's arm would have bounced off hers.

"You again!" was her way of greeting.

"For the last time, I promise," I said. "May I come in?"

She considered it for a moment, then almost imperceptibly nodded her head and stepped aside. I noticed that Fluffy had come to the large foyer too, doubtless to see who was crazy enough to visit her owner.

"Well?" Velma demanded.

"It looks like the police are going to be able to arrest Big Jim's killer," I told her.

"I don't give a shit about that!" she snapped. "Where's the money he stole from the Bolivians?"

"The police will have three of the diamonds soon."

"That's three million, maybe a little more," she said. "Where's the rest?"

I shook my head. "That's three hundred thousand, maybe a little less."

"What kind of bullshit is this? We both know he stole millions from the Bolivian mob!"

"Maybe he overestimated," I answered. "But two reputable jewelers have valued them at a hundred thousand apiece, tops."

"What the fuck are you trying to get away with?" she demanded.

"Not a thing. You hired me to find the cat," I said. "Well, the diamonds. I've found three of them. The killer has the other six, and he's so far in debt that he's probably sold them already. The seventh is in a ring he gave his girlfriend. You *might* be able to get that one back. I'm just here to report that the job you paid me for is done."

"Who's the killer?" she said.

I figured if I told her, she'd walk over to Delahunt's house, kill him if he was there, rip the joint apart and maybe kill Mrs. Delahunt if she got in the way, and find a way to blame me for her being there at all.

"The police will let you know as soon as they've arrested him," I said.

"You are a goddamned fucking liar!" she screamed. "We both know those diamonds are worth a million apiece! Jim had been ripping those assholes off for years. He could have hidden a million every three months!"

"The cops will have their hands on three of the diamonds in a few days," I said. "If you don't believe me, maybe you'll believe them."

"You kept the real ones and substituted some cheap ones!"

"They'll match the descriptions on your insurance policy," I said.

"You're *all* liars!" she bellowed. "You, the cops, the insurance company, all of you!"

She stamped her foot down and managed to land it on Fluffy's tail. The cat screeched in pain and surprise.

"Here!" she said, reaching down, grabbing Fluffy up by the scruff of the neck, and hurling her at me with a motion that would have been the envy of Roger Clemens.

I caught her against my stomach, let out an "Oof!" and tried to think of what to do next.

"I never want to see either of you again!" she shrieked. "Now get the fuck out of my house!"

I considered putting Fluffy down, but I decided no one, not even a cat, should have to live in the same house as Velma, so I opened the door with my free hand, carried the cat out to the car, deposited her in the backseat, and backed out of the driveway before Velma remembered that Palanto had a gun and went looking for it.

The cat meowed unhappily all the way home. I found a parking place just a couple of doors down from my apartment, picked the cat up, climbed up the stairs, and was about to unlock the door when I realized who was waiting on the other side of it.

Marlowe had squatter's rights on that apartment, and he probably outweighed Fluffy by a good five pounds, which may not have been much difference when Ali fought Frazier, but it gave him a 50 percent body weight advantage.

Well, I'd just have to use a firm hand and keep an eye on him. Fluffy hadn't asked to be literally thrown out of her home, and I decided it was my job to keep Marlowe from ripping her to shreds until I could find a new home for her.

I needn't have worried. I opened the door, stepped inside, set her on the floor, and said, "Marlowe, say hello to your new roomie."

He took one look at her and spent the rest of the night hiding under my bed.

28.

Marlowe was still under the bed when I got up about eight o'clock. As for Fluffy, she was curled up on his favorite couch cushion, looking for all the world like she owned the place.

"Okay," I muttered. "I don't know much about cats, but one thing I do know is they use litter boxes. Hold yourself in check another twenty minutes."

I got dressed, put on my coat, and walked a couple of blocks to the little mom-and-pop grocery store, picked up a bag of cat litter and a plastic box, then let them sell me a scoop to clear the litter out of the box, and a couple of minutes later I was back in the apartment, pouring litter into the box and sticking it under the bathroom sink.

I picked Fluffy up, carried her to the bathroom, set her down in the box, and waited.

She stared right back, stood there for a minute, then jumped out, walked back to the couch with all the dignity she could muster, and hopped back up onto the cushion.

I figured as long as I still had my coat on, I might as well take Marlowe for his walk, since to the best of my knowledge dogs didn't use litter boxes. I had to reach under the bed and drag him out. Then he practically pulled me out the door and down the stairs. At first I thought he had to go, but when we got outside he just stood there, and I realized what he really wanted to do was get away from Fluffy.

I walked him to Mrs. Garabaldi's where force of habit took over, he watered her petunias, and we headed back home. This time he didn't make a beeline for the space under the bed but just sat in the farthest corner of the living room and stared at Fluffy.

"You know," I said aloud, staring at the cat, "if you're going to stick around for any length of time, you need a better name. A manly, macho private eye can't have a pet called Fluffy. A dame, maybe, but not a cat." I considered my options. "He's named after Philip Marlowe, but you're the wrong color to be Sam Spade. Besides, if I call you Spade, some of the black guys at the Twenty Yard Line might take serious offense." I stared at her further, and finally it came to me. "You're a female, and Samantha's a name for a female. And since we're going to be living together, at least for a while, that's too formal, so I think I'll call you Sam. How does that sit with you?"

She opened one eye and stared at me. *That's fine. I can ignore you when you call me Sam just as easily as when you call me Fluffy.*

Marlowe gave me an *I could have told you so* look, and then I checked my watch and realized that they'd be releasing Mela in about forty-five minutes, and I didn't want him going anywhere but to the Cincinnati police with me.

I opened a can of sardines that was old enough to grow a beard and left it on the kitchen counter where Marlowe couldn't reach it. I figured Sam could smell them, and when she got hungry enough she'd make her way back there and grab a little breakfast or lunch, and of course she could share Marlowe's water bowl.

Then I was out the door, and a minute later I was driving across the Ohio River to St. Elizabeth's. I parked, went in, got a fierce glare from the receptionist I'd spoken to yesterday, and was about to ask about Mela when he approached from wherever he'd been waiting.

"Hi," I said. "How are you today?"

"Fine," he said. "It's really just a scratch." Suddenly he smiled. "I hope it leaves a scar, though."

"Oh?" I said. "Why?"

"I have an older brother who fought in Vietnam. He took a bullet in the leg, and for the next twenty years every time our family, which is quite large, had a reunion, every one of the kids nagged and nagged until he showed them his scar." He paused. "I was 4-F." He patted his arm gingerly. "Now I finally have a wound to show them."

"If I'd known it meant that much to you, I'd have shot you myself," I said, and he chuckled. "I suppose they confiscated the box?"

He nodded. "You told me they would."

"Okay, we're a day late, but they still want to see you," I said. "I'll drive us over."

"Will this take very long?" he asked.

"They'll probably be done with you in an hour," I said. "But of course it'll take them a few days to get the diamonds—after all, two guys were killed in Covington because of them. Still, the two departments work pretty well together, and since there's no one left alive to charge with murder and there's a murder case pending across the river, I think the diamonds should be in Cincinnati in, oh, maybe a week."

"I can save you a return trip and have my wife pick me up," he offered.

"The cops will take you back," I said. "You're only there because they want to see you, and since you're coming willingly and saving them a ton of interstate paperwork, they'll be happy to do it." I paused. "At least, they'll *look* happy."

"The man who yelled at you to duck," said Mela as we walked to the car. "Was he your partner?"

"In a way," I said.

"How is he?"

"Dead."

"I'm sorry."

"So am I," I said. "But if he hadn't been backing me up, you and I would be lying side by side in the morgue."

He shook his head. "All because Abner stole some diamonds."

"All because he stole some diamonds from a man he'd just killed," I said.

He rubbed his face with his delicate hands. "It's all too much for me. Jewelers are conditioned to worry about robbery, not murder."

We crossed the combined I-71/I-75 bridge to Ohio, and a couple of minutes later I parked at headquarters and escorted Mela into the building and up to Jim Simmons's office.

"Good morning, Eli," said Simmons, getting to his feet and turning to Mela. "And you must be Mr. Mela. I hope you're okay?"

Mela nodded. "Just a scratch, thanks to Mr. Paxton and his partner."

"Partner?" said Simmons curiously, looking at me.

"Friend," I said.

"I was sorry to hear about him," said Simmons.

"While I'm thinking of it," I said, "when the diamonds are finally returned to Velma, I want the finder's fee to go to his family."

Simmons smiled. "First we got to find them."

"Orestes?" I said. "Tell the lieutenant what's in the custody of the Covington police."

"Three diamonds worth perhaps a hundred thousand each, possibly a little less. I don't think any jeweler will argue with an estimate of eighty-five to ninety."

"And these are the diamonds you were bringing to me yesterday when the shooting started?"

He nodded his head. "Yes."

"Exactly how did you come by these diamonds, Mr. Mela?" asked Simmons.

"They were part of a group of ten that were brought to me last week by Abner Delahunt."

"Where are the other seven?"

Mela shrugged. "I can only give you hearsay. I set one of them into a ring that I am told Mr. Delahunt gave to a lady friend, but I have no proof of that. And Mr. Delahunt took the other six back, and I have not seem him or them since then."

"Okay," said Simmons, "that jibes with what Eli told us. We've already confiscated the ring. Are you willing to identify it when we ask you to?"

"Certainly."

"One last question: Are you willing to be deposed?"

"Deposed?" repeated Mela.

Simmons nodded. "You'll be escorted to another room, accompanied by two members of my staff, and they'll ask you to repeat your story in front of a recorder, a video camera, and a steno—and after a stenographer types it up you'll be asked to sign it. Do you have a problem with any facet of that?"

"No, sir, I do not," said Mela.

"Good." Simmons pressed a button on his desk, and a moment later a plainclothes cop opened the door. "Tom, will you and Barry please escort Mr. Mela down the hall and take his deposition?"

Tom nodded. "And afterward?"

"He's free to go. In fact, find him a ride home. If one of our men isn't heading that way, get him a cab."

"Yes, sir," he said, leading Mela out of the office.

"Well," said Simmons, leaning back in his chair, "you delivered him. And when you didn't show yesterday, before I got word about what had happened, I brought in the girl just to be on the safe side."

"Mitzi Cramer?"

He nodded. "That's when we impounded the ring." Suddenly he smiled. "What she's doing outside of *Playboy* or *Penthouse* I don't know." The grin got bigger. "You wouldn't believe how many cops offered to take her home."

I chuckled at that. "So what's next?"

"We bring Delahunt in, of course."

"Today?"

"If he's home or at work, yes. If not, we issue a B.O.L.O. for him. I think we've got the goods on him. Maybe not for murder, but surely for stealing the diamonds."

"I've never even seen the man," I said. "You mind if I stick around?"

"No problem," he said. "He'll be lawyered up, of course. And you can't sit in the interrogation room, but you can watch and listen through the one-way glass."

"Sounds good," I said. "I'm going to go out and grab a quick lunch. No way you bring him in before I get back."

"Hell, it'll take a couple of hours. You know he's not talking to anyone until he's got his lawyer at his side."

"That gives me time to head up to Rascal's," I said.

"The deli?"

I nodded. "The best in town. Doesn't everyone want blintzes and chopped liver right before nailing a killer?"

"Some of us prefer lox and knishes," he said.

"Hint taken," I replied. "I'll bring some back for you."

"You're a good man, Eli," he said. "Even if I do have to buy the tickets for the Bengals game."

"I hope it's that easy," I said. "But let's get him to confess first."

"Let's also keep it legal and un-include you from the 'let's,'" he said. "Now go. I'm gonna be starved in two hours."

I went.

29.

I hit some traffic coming back from Rascal's, and I got to headquarters about forty minutes later than I'd planned to. And on the way in I almost bumped into Tyler Grange, wearing one of his usual twelve-hundred-dollar suits and a pair of four-hundred-dollar shoes.

"Hello, Eli," he said. "Long time no see."

"Hi, Tyler," I replied. "Here to defend the meek and disposed, as usual?"

He gave me a deprecating little chuckle. "Just here for a deposition."

"Would I be dead wrong if I suggested that you're representing Abner Delahunt?" I asked.

He looked surprised. "You know Abner?"

"Never met him in my life," I said truthfully.

"Well, I don't know how you come by your information," he said, frowning, "but yes, I'm representing him."

"Can I give you a little hint?"

"Sure," he said with a phony smile. "Innocent or guilty?"

"That's up to a jury to decide," I said. "If it gets that far."

"That's why he's got *me*," said Grange. "To make sure if it gets that far that he's innocent of whatever he's charged with." He paused. "And your hint about this man you've never met?"

"Don't charge him more than minimum wage, Tyler."

He frowned, "I beg your pardon?"

"He's dead broke."

The frown increased. "What makes you think so?"

"Just a hunch," I said.

"Well, you're wrong. The man has a dozen real estate offices."

"Whatever you say," I replied. *Besides, it'll do you good to do some pro bono work.*

"I have to go," he said. "I have some business to transact."

I shook his hand but didn't wish him luck. He went off toward the holding cells, which meant that Delahunt was already in custody, and I brought Simmons his lunch.

"Thanks," he said.

"I ran into Tyler Grange down the hall," I told him.

"Yeah, he's representing Delahunt," answered Simmons. He frowned. "He's damned good. He could make this much more difficult."

"You've got everything you need," I said. "Mela, Mitzi, and the diamonds. Or you soon *will* have it, anyway."

"Oh, we can prove he stole the diamonds. Proving that he murdered Palanto will be harder."

"He's new to this," I said. "You'll trip him up."

"I hope so."

"I wish I could sit in on it," I said.

He shook his head. "You know you can't. Settle for watching and listening from the next room."

"So who's going to be questioning him?"

"Wayne Perin's our best at it," he answered. "I've filled him in on all the details, and he's spoken to Mela and Mitzi. And I'll probably sit in on it too."

"I hope you nail the bastard," I said. "Originally all I wanted was to find the diamonds, but they're worth nothing to me now, and a man died saving my life."

"Delahunt didn't kill him," noted Simmons.

"If Delahunt didn't kill Palanto and steal the diamonds, then Sorrentino would have gone back to Chicago."

"I've said it before, Eli. You've got interesting friends."

He unwrapped his lunch and started to eat it. He'd just finished it off when Wayne Perin knocked on the door, stuck his head in, and said, "Ready, Jim?"

Simmons nodded. "I'm on my way."

He got up, walked to the door, gestured for me to accompany him, and walked to the nearest interrogation room.

"In there," he said, pointing to the next door. I walked over to it and entered, and found an empty chair next to a video and sound technician, a stenographer, and a couple of detectives I'd seen that first night at Palanto's house.

"Before we begin," said Tyler Grange, who was sitting next to a balding, very nervous little man who fit Delahunt's description, "my client freely admits that he took Malcolm Pepperidge's cat and removed ten diamonds from its collar, diamonds to which he had no legal claim."

"Yes, we know," said Perin. "We have depositions on record from Orestes Mela, the jeweler who removed the diamonds from the cat's collar, set one in a ring that he gave to a Miss Mitzi Cramer that is now in our possession, and bought three of them, which he has since turned over. The other six were returned to Mr. Delahunt, who is doubtless anxious to tell us where they are."

"I don't know," said Delahunt.

Perin smiled. "You *lost* six valuable diamonds in a week's time?"

Delahunt shook his head. "No, I didn't *lose* them. I *sold* them."

"My client will be happy to provide you with the details," added Grange.

"And the bills of sale?" asked Simmons.

Delahunt whispered into Grange's ear.

"These were *informal* transactions," said Grange.

"So the buyer knew they were hot," said Perin.

"Yes, we would so characterize them," replied Grange.

"But of course, formal or informal, selling stolen merchandise is a felony," continued Perin. "Now let's talk about Mr. Palanto . . . excuse me, Mr. Pepperidge."

"What would you like to know?" asked Grange smoothly.

"Personally, I'd like to know why Mr. Delahunt killed him."

"I didn't!" yelled Delahunt.

"Come on, Mr. Delahunt," said Perin. "The cat was there when the servants left for the night. The cat and Mr. Pepperidge were both alive and well, and both in the house, when Mrs. Pepperidge went off to play bridge. And Mr. Pepperidge was dead and the cat was missing when Mrs. Pepperidge returned home. You entered the house, with or without Pepperidge's knowledge, while she was gone, killed him, and absconded with the cat. What other possible explanation can there be?"

"That's not what happened!" yelled Delahunt.

"Of course it is," said Perin.

"Look, I've already admitted I stole the diamonds!" said Delahunt, sweat starting to appear on his forehead. "Malcolm Pepperidge was a friend. We golfed together. We had the occasional meal together. Hell, he loaned me money a few months ago when my business took a turn for the worse." He pulled out a handkerchief. "In fact, that's why I went to his house that night—to arrange another loan. But when I got there the front door was unlocked. I went up to his study, but he wasn't there. I felt an odd breeze coming from his bedroom, so I walked over there and saw him lying dead on that balcony. There was no question that he was dead. He'd once told me that he'd had some valuable diamonds put on the cat's collar as a gift to his wife. I needed money, and I lost my head and picked up the cat, and then I got the hell out of there."

"Why was the cat found twenty miles away the next day?" asked Simmons.

"There was so much snow," said Delahunt. "I thought if I let it out of my house, it wouldn't go anywhere, and I couldn't have it found there. And I heard the police sirens—I was just three houses away—so I knew I couldn't take the cat back to the Pepperidge house, not with a dead body lying there on the balcony. So I waited until the major streets were plowed the next morning, drove it out to the city limits, and turned it loose."

"That's a good story," acknowledged Perin.

"It's the truth."

"No, it's not," said Perin. "You rang the doorbell or knocked on the door, Pepperidge let you in, you went up to his bedroom and asked for a loan, he probably said not until you paid back the last one, he'd been checking the storm and the stars when you arrived, and he went out to take another look. And that's when you shot him."

"No!" shouted Delahunt. "I took the cat, yes—but I didn't shoot anyone."

"Yes, you did," said Perin. "Three shots, right between the shoulder blades."

"No!"

"Yes," persisted Perin. "Three quick shots, and it was all over, and given the weather no one had any windows open, so no one could hear either shot."

"That's a lie!" yelled Delahunt as Grange tried to calm him down.

"Come on, Mr. Delahunt," said Perin. "We've got all three bullets. Sooner or later we're going to find your gun, and ballistics is going to match them to it."

"But I only shot him twice!" cried Delahunt, then realized what he'd said and buried his face in his hands.

Simmons turned to where he knew I was watching and gave me a thumbs-up.

Twenty minutes later we were back in his office.

"I told you Wayne was our best," said Simmons happily.

"Tyler Grange is going to say you tricked it out of him."

"We did," answered Simmons. "But it's on record, and it's the truth. Besides, you know our Tyler. Guilty doesn't bother him, but broke and guilty does. I think he'll find some reason to drop the case any hour now." He smiled. "This will be one time I'll be happy to treat you to dinner at the Precinct."

"I'm glad we nailed him, and I'm glad it's over," I said. "I haven't made a penny since Velma gave me that retainer to find the cat. It's time I got back to being a detective." I paused, then added: "Well, a paid one."

"Whatever became of the damned cat?"

"Don't ask," I said.

30.

I stopped at the Covington morgue and made arrangements to ship Sorrentino's body home to Chicago. One phone call to his boss, and everything was paid for. I stopped by my office for the first time in a week, picked up the mail—mostly ads, a few bills, nothing else—and while I was there I called the insurance company. Simmons had already confirmed my claim before I made it, and a fee for four diamonds was earmarked for Sorrentino's daughters.

Then I drove home, parked the car, and entered the apartment building. Mrs. Cominsky was waiting for me.

"I'm afraid to go out on the street," she said.

"I don't blame you," I replied. "Stick to the sidewalks."

"Damn it, you know what I mean. There are all these sex-mad creatures out there." She paused for emphasis. "Of both sexes."

"The mail has to be slowing down," I said. "I mean, it's been about a week."

She frowned. "Yes, it has."

"That should make you happy."

"You know what I think?" she said.

"Probably not," I answered. "What *do* you think?"

"I think we should take out another ad."

"Too late," I said. "The case is closed."

She shook her head. "I don't care about that case. There are so many perverts out there! We should make something up and ask for replies, and then, when we've received the worst of them, turn 'em over to the vice squad."

"You don't need me for that," I told her. "Just take out the ad, collect your perverts, and contact the cops."

"Well, maybe not right away."

"You don't want to take out the ad right away?"

She shook her head impatiently. "Oh, I'll take it out this week. I mean that I might not turn over the worst letters right away. I might give them innocent replies and see if they write again. Then we know we've got 'em."

"Sounds good to me," I said, edging toward my apartment door. "And you might think of getting a post office box so no one knows your address."

"I'm way ahead of you," she said proudly. "I got one this morning." She paused thoughtfully. "I wonder why no one else ever thought of this?"

"There just aren't that many original thinkers around," I answered, and made it to my door. I slid the key in the lock and was inside before she could tell me anything more about her correspondents.

Marlowe was lying on one of the couch cushions. Sam was on the other. Each opened one eye, said, *Oh, it's you* and went back to sleep.

I stared at them for a moment. A week ago I thought I might be turning in ten million dollars' worth of diamonds for the reward. At the very least I thought I'd have enough to buy the Ford a new transmission. I'd been lied to, I'd been shot at, and all I had to show for it was a non-descript cat that was too bored by my homecoming to open both eyes.

I figured I might as well take Marlowe out for a walk before it got too much colder and barely made it outside before Mrs. Cominsky could tell me all about the perverts she was going to nail with her brilliant scheme.

As we walked, I wondered how Delahunt felt. Trapped, of course, and surely facing life, at the very least. But I wonder if he felt cheated, not that he'd been caught, but that he'd bought Palanto's lie about ten million, that he'd killed him for diamonds that were worth a million.

Then I remembered that it wasn't Delahunt who thought there was ten million on that collar. It was Sorrentino, and since he'd gone there just to make sure that his mob and its former financial advisor were still friends, why the hell would he lie?

Well, he wouldn't, of course. But how the hell could he be so wrong about what they were worth? I had the damned collar at home in a drawer. I could see that there was only room for ten diamonds on it. Mela hadn't lied, and Mela and Monroe had both agreed on the value.

I shrugged. It was something I'd never know the answer to. The only answer that mattered was that I didn't get a penny for finding the diamonds. At least Sorrentino's kids would benefit, maybe get into a nice college, maybe someday forget what their father did for a living.

Marlowe got cold and started dragging me back to the apartment. When we got there, I'd swear Sam hadn't moved a muscle. I checked the kitchen. She'd eaten half the sardines, so I left them out in case she was inclined to grab a late-night snack. I noticed that she'd used the litter box too. I'd have cleaned it out, but I didn't know where to dump it, so I decided to wait a day or two while I considered the problem.

It was Cary Grant night on TCM, and I forced my way between Marlowe and Sam, and half-watched and half-snoozed through *Mr. Blandings Builds His Dream House* and *The Bachelor and the Bobby-Soxer*. Marlowe started growling when *Father Goose* came on, which was either a critical response or just a serious distaste for color on the TV. AMC had something in color, too, so I turned the set off, walked him one last time, and went to bed.

In the morning I had to get out from under a pile of animals. I shaved, decided it was past time to shower, put on some clean clothes to prove to myself that I was ready to be a paid detective again, and put a leash on Marlowe.

It was a chilly morning. We walked briskly to Mrs. Garabaldi's, watered the grave of her dead petunias (which would bloom again in spring, provided he didn't drown them), and made it home just as a light snow began falling.

When I got to my door I ran into Mrs. Cominsky, who was on her way down for the mail. She was at least an hour early, but I imagined her just standing there eagerly awaiting the next pile of letters from the mailman—and as I unlocked and opened my door, Sam darted out into the hallway. I grabbed her by the scruff of the neck, tossed her back inside, and slammed the door.

"A cat?" said Mrs. Cominsky furiously. "You've got a cat now?"

"Temporarily," I said. Then: "This is the one our ruse was about."

"She's part of our case?" she replied, her face brightening. "That's okay then." She paused thoughtfully. "You know, you really ought to get her a license. One of these days she could sneak out past you, and there goes our case—poof! Up the river."

"She's already got a license," I said. "I'll put it on her when I get inside."

"Good idea," she said.

Marlowe looked up at Mrs. Cominsky, barked once, and wagged his tail.

"Ugly little brute," she said, and continued down to the mailboxes.

I went inside, took Marlowe's leash off, made the bed for the first time all week, and went over to the drawer where I'd put Sam's collar.

I pulled it out, looked at the tag, and frowned. If she actually did sneak out, anyone who found her would check the number on the collar with the animal warden or SPCA or whoever the hell gave out cat licenses, and return her to Velma, which was a fate no cat or person should have to undergo.

I pulled down the phone book. I couldn't find animal wardens listed, but there was a big boxed listing for the SPCA.

"Yes?" said a woman's voice at the other end.

"Hello," I said. "I've just been given a cat as a present."

"How very nice for you both," she said.

"Thank you," I said. "Anyway, I would never want to do anything that wasn't in accordance with the law, so I want to know how much a cat license costs and where I can pick one up."

And thirty seconds later I shocked the dear woman by yelling, "*Shit!*" as the last piece of the puzzle fell into place.

31.

I walked into Jim Simmons's office and sat down across his desk from him.

"Whatever you did," he said, "you look pretty damned proud of yourself."

"I think I've solved it, but I need verification."

"What the hell are you talking about, Eli?"

"The missing money in the Palanto case," I said.

"What missing money?" he shot back with a puzzled expression. "We've got four of the diamonds, and we're tracing the other six."

"Peanuts," I said.

"I'll say it again," replied Simmons. "What are you talking about?"

"Val Sorrentino was here to make sure that Palanto was loyal to his former employers, that he wasn't going to testify against them in their upcoming trial in Chicago."

"I know."

"He paid a visit to Palanto, and Palanto gave him the assurances he wanted."

"What does this have to do with anything?"

"Palanto left Chicago with a clean sheet and the mob's blessing. He made them rich and never stole a penny from them. He came here, changed his name, and lived like a retired millionaire. But he *wasn't* retired. He did some work for the Bolivian cartel."

"I know all this."

"And he skimmed ten million from them. That's what he told Sorrentino."

"Eli, we've searched every account, every safe deposit box, every mutual fund, everything he had. There's a million dollars in diamonds, but he bought them legitimately. There just isn't any missing ten million."

I grinned at him.

"What the hell do you think you know?"

"Velma knew he had ten million too," I said. "She just didn't know where it was." I paused. "Neither did I." I gave him another grin. "Until today."

"I hope to hell you're enjoying this," he said irritably.

"I am," I said.

"So where is it?"

"I've been sitting on it for three days."

"I'm tired of asking," said Simmons.

"Okay," I said. "Mela gave me the cat's collar, with all the diamonds missing. Nothing on it but the license. Velma gave me the cat. Damned near threw it at me. So I took it home until I could figure out what to do with it."

"Okay, so you've got a cat."

"This morning it tried to sneak out of the apartment, and my land-lady suggested that I get a license for it in case it ever makes it past the front door. I already *had* a license on its collar, but I figured if someone found it they'd check the license and return it to Velma, who would probably cook it for supper. So I called the SPCA to find out where to get a new license for it."

I paused and gave him one last grin.

"Okay," said Simmons. "What's the punch line?"

"Jim, Ohio doesn't issue license tags for cats, just for dogs!"

He stared at me. "You're sure about this?"

"I just got it from the SPCA, and then I double-checked with the animal shelter where I found the cat." I pulled the collar out of my pocket and tossed it on his desk. "I don't know what the hell the numbers on the plate mean, but I'll bet you dollars to donuts they lead to ten million bucks!"

"Jesus!" he said, picking it up and staring at the tag.

"Mean anything to you?"

He read it aloud. "39ZK30126. Nope, makes no sense to me. But *someone* in the building will know."

And an hour later, Deborah Oakes of the Bank Fraud Division *did* know.

"Very clever," she said, when she invited us to her office. "The 39 identifies the account holder as an American, the ZK stands for Zürcher Kantonalbank, one of Switzerland's largest banks, and the 30126 is his account number."

"What has he got in the account?" I asked.

She turned to Simmons questioningly, and he nodded his approval.

"As of this morning," she replied, "he has nine million, six hundred, and forty-three thousand, two hundred, and eleven dollars and nine cents. That's based on today's exchange rates, of course."

"Son of a bitch!" I said. "I *knew* that had to be it!"

"Thank you, Deborah," said Simmons. He took the collar and tag back from her, and then he and I returned to his office.

"The press is going to call you brilliant, Eli," he said. "We won't tell them it was dumb luck and a wandering cat."

"Tell 'em anything you want," I said. "I have to compute my finder's fee."

"For the diamonds?" he said, frowning. "I thought that was earmarked for Sorrentino's daughters."

"All right, my reward, then," I said.

"For what?"

"For nine and a half million dollars," I said.

"Eli," he said seriously, "you're not thinking this through."

It was my turn to frown. "In what way?"

"It's probably stolen money," said Simmons. "But it wasn't stolen from the United States. Also, for all we know, that particular part of Palanto's fortune *was* totally legit. He'd made some very successful investments over the years, and he wasn't a pauper when he moved here."

"Come on, Jim," I said. "We both know it's the money he skimmed from the Bolivians."

"From a Bolivian drug cartel," he replied. "If anyone's offering a reward for a return of the money, it's them. But do you really want to deal with them after you got two of their hit men deported and a third killed?"

"I know that the US government gives a reward," I insisted stubbornly.

He stared at me sadly. "First, you have to prove the money in question was stolen from the Bolivians and not legitimately earned through investments. Second, you have to prove that it wasn't Velma's money that he was keeping or investing for her. Third, by the time the government actually agrees, if they ever do, you're going to be an old, old man."

I was silent for a long minute. Finally I looked across the desk at him.

"The Bengals had better win," I said, "and that had better be the best steak I've ever tasted."

32.

I was in a lousy mood when I got home, and it didn't get much better over the next few hours. I'd solved a murder and got nothing for it. I'd found a million dollars in missing diamonds and got nothing for it. I'd found almost ten million dollars hidden in a Swiss bank account and got nothing for it. All I'd gotten for the whole thing was half a transmission and a cat that had no more use for humans than Marlowe did.

I went out to a chili joint for dinner, brought back a cheese coney for each of the animals, and sat down on the couch to watch some TV while they were chowing down. I was hoping for a Bogey festival, or at least a Jimmy Cagney one. But it was as if someone at Turner Classic Movies had been spying on me and had a sardonic sense of humor. It was Animal Night, and as Sam ambled in and jumped up on her cushion and tried to push me onto the other one, and Marlowe jumped on *his* cushion and started pushing me back, we were treated to *Rhubarb*, about a cat that inherits a baseball team, which was certainly more productive than a cat that loses a ten-million-dollar collar; and *Lassie Come Home*, which was a few steps ahead of a dog that reluctantly leaves his couch very briefly three or four times a day.

I fell asleep ten minutes into the first one. I don't know how long I slept there on the couch, but life became appreciably better when Bettie Page started purring in my left ear while a magically youthful Sophia Loren passionately kissed my right.

Then the dog and cat movies were over, *The Black Stallion* came on, Bettie began running moist sandpaper in my left ear while Sophia started barking in my right, and I was back in the real world again.

ABOUT THE AUTHOR

Photo by Hugette

Mike Resnick is the author of the previous Eli Paxton mysteries *Dog in the Manger* and *The Trojan Colt*. The all-time leading award winner, living or dead, for short science fiction, he has won five Hugos (from a record thirty-six nominations), plus other major awards in the United States, France, Spain, Croatia, Poland, and Japan. He is the author of over seventy novels, more than two hundred fifty stories, and three screenplays, and he has edited forty-one anthologies. His work has been translated into twenty-five languages.